CW00550972

Cover design by Jessica Allain, Enchanted Whispers

Interior design by Zoe Parker

Edited by Cassandra Fear

If you are unable to order this book from your local bookseller, you may contact the author at info@authormayadaniels.com or visit the website

www.authormayadaniels.com

The Devil is in the Details

Maya Daniels

Chapter One

Helena

One week ago

The city passes in a blur as I stare out the window, not seeing a single thing as my mind replays the last few hours yet again. *What if's* have never been my favorite to start with, but I can't help thinking that if we'd done anything differently, then maybe, just maybe, I wouldn't have this gnawing feeling that my life took a nosedive off a cliff and it's headed straight for the jutting rocks at the bottom. *What did I miss?* Questions rattle in my brain, causing my temples to pound with their own heartbeat.

"This should be our last stop before we head back."

George yanks me out of my thoughts when his deep, rusty voice echoes in my ears. I hate the earpieces they make us wear, even though I know how useful they are. Well, useful for the rest of them, anyway; I'm more than capable of taking care of myself. There's no reason for him to use it because we're all sitting in his car, but he likes being a jerk. Glaring at the back of his head, I fight the urge to smack his head on the steering wheel he's clutching in his paw-sized hands like the thing is trying to escape. If you call him out on it, you'll have to listen to lectures on how he makes sure the equipment is working, so the rest of us just grind our teeth and say nothing. There's five of us in the car. Jared, Cass, and Amanda act like it doesn't bother them, but I see their jaws ticking in the occasional light we pass.

Lost in my thoughts, I am enjoying the quiet after our last stop, especially since one of the abominations managed to draw blood before I sent him where he belongs. We are the chosen hunters in North America that protect humans from all things that go bump in the night. We are the shadows of society, members of the Order. Entrusted and blessed by the Archangels themselves—or so we are told—we mostly hunt demons, with an occasional vamp or shifter mixed in.

Our last stop, an hour ago, was a suburb of Atlanta,

Georgia, where three demons had nested and terrorized humans for over a month. Possessing them, they jumped from one body to the next and turned a lovely, quiet neighborhood into something from nightmares. Out of nowhere, domestic violence blossomed, neighbors killed each other, and fires and break-ins happened every night. It put a red dot on the area, and we were dispatched to investigate.

Needless to say, the demons are no more, and I pray that the neighborhood goes back to the idyllic picture the lawns and homes suggested it used to be.

Lifting my arm towards the window, I check to see if the scratch one of the demons left by raking its claws over me has healed. Only thin pink lines are still visible, but those will be gone by the time I take a shower and wash the grime and blood off me. There will be nothing left, not even a scar, but I remember the demon's words clearly: "Soon all of you will regret getting involved in things that you know nothing about." Its raspy voice rattles through my brain.

All of us are blessed with fast healing, longer lifespans, speed, and strength. I would like to think I'm still human, but with each new day after my eighteenth birthday three years ago, I doubt that statement more and more. To make matters worse, I'm more different than the rest of them. My sixth sense is like a GPS for evil, even when the others can't see demons or any of the other evil creatures that plague humanity.

It's almost as if evil calls to me, daring me to find it.

One thing I've never told anyone is that when that feeling starts inside my chest, it's like I'm about to receive the greatest gift of my life. Excitement and giddiness course through my veins, making me sick to my stomach. It should feel repulsive, yet it doesn't. I've lied to everyone I call friends and family, telling them that it's a sickening feeling because I don't want anyone doubting my loyalties. My conscience on this matter is not clear.

"It should be around the corner." George speaks through the earpiece again, making me physically flinch. Instinctively my fist goes up, heading straight for the back of his head. Unnerved by the entire night, I'm barely able to control the anger still pulsing through me, and he's pushing it. I know because his dark eyes lock with mine in the rearview mirror every time he does it daring me to say something.

Fast as lightning, Amanda grabs my forearm, and her bright pink nails dig into my flesh. "That's good! We can get it done and go home," she says, emphasizing *home* like she's not glaring at me in the back seat.

Amanda's pink pixie cut hair is styled in teal-tipped spikes on top of her head. Large brown eyes shaded with glittery eyeshadow and sparkly mascara on her long lashes blink contrasting against her porcelain face. She looks almost like a doll. Like those anime characters that she loves so much. We've been best friends ever since I can remember, and no one knows me as well as she does.

No wonder she snatched my arm before my fist connected with the back of George's head.

"Yes, I'm actually looking forward to the 'go home' part!" Cass snickers, smacking Jared on the shoulder, making his body twist in the passenger seat to look at her over his shoulder. His blue eyes light up and he gives her a beaming smile when she grins at him.

"Oh boy! I'm gonna be sick." Amanda groans, rolling her eyes dramatically. "The lovey-dovey googly eyes crap makes me sick." She turns to me again, pretending to gag. My arm slowly lowers, and she stops digging her nails into my flesh, petting my forearm gently before releasing it.

"Yeah." Taking a deep breath, I lean back in my seat and turn to look out the window. "Go in, get out, go home, and no lovey-dovey googly eyes. It works for me."

"Of course, it works for you, Hel! You wouldn't know what googly eyes were if they hit you in the face." Amanda giggles, smacking my thigh with the back of her hand. "Ouch! Move those guns, would you?" She sneers at my weapons as if it's their fault she hit her hand on them.

"Leave the girls alone! They're fine just where they are." Petting them affectionately, I scowl back at her.

The SUV makes a left turn, and we forget all about the conversation. All the streetlights are broken, leaving the street pitch black. Our headlights light up a quarter of it revealing a sight that will haunt me for months. Bodies with missing parts are haphazardly tossed around like a zombie Apocalypse movie set. My stomach clenches and my entire body coils up, ready to fight as energy rushes through me. Tension rises inside the car as the three of us lean forward from the back seat to see better. This is not something we see every day, even in our line of work. The abominations are getting bolder by the minute, but we've never seen anything so messed up until now. At least it can't get worse than this. George flicks on his high beams, and we take a sharp, collective intake of breath at the gruesome view revealed in front of us.

I was wrong. It can get worse.

Crouched above dozens of piles of dead humans are gray, wrinkled demons, their arrow-pointed tails flicking like cats' while they tear the flesh off the bones they clutch in their claw-tipped hands. Their heads snap in our direction, revealing red, glowing eyes and gaping mouths full of razor-sharp shark teeth. Looking like aliens with only eyes and a mouth, blood drips down their grotesque faces as they hiss in unison. Everyone else in the car freezes, but the anger that I've been fighting all night churns and splutters like a volcano in my chest. There is no way my team can fight this without a scratch. I must stand between them if my friends are to survive. Pushing the door open, I jump out of the car.

"Hel, no!" Amanda's scream pierces the night, but I slam the door in her face.

Pulling both of my revolvers out of their holsters, the

usual calm engulfs me like a blanket. Feeling their comforting weight in my hands, I smile at the hissing abominations that turn towards me.

"Playtime, motherfuckers!"

All the abominations spring into action with an eerie screech. Like mice trying to escape a flood, a horde of them bound in my direction. The high beams of the car at my back make it easier to pick them off one by one. The sound of the gunshots energizes me with its beauty. The demons drop one by one like rocks, their bodies causing those behind to trip and roll on the cracked, uneven concrete of the street.

Shadows move at the corner of my eye as the rest of my team joins me. Blades, throwing stars, and knives fly in the air as they take down more demons. Shouts and hoots sound above my shots as we add more bodies to this street of nightmares, where so many unfortunate innocent humans lost their lives tonight.

The pink scars on my forearm throb for no reason, making me hesitate long enough to realize the demons are not trying to fight or defend themselves. They are dying in their attempts to get to me. My team spreads around me like a circle, guarding my back while I'm in shock at the horrifying thought. I almost drop my guns, which makes rage bubble in my chest. None of them will escape tonight.

The haunting screeches don't stop until the early hours. It's a night the five of us will remember for as long as we live. It's a night that changed everything and destroyed the life I have built for myself for over twenty years. I just pray that my team forgets that none of the abominations tried to kill me. Instead, they died trying to capture me alive. Too bad for them I'm never an easy prey.

Chapter Two

Eric…

Looking at the old man standing in front of me wringing his hands behind his back, I smell his righteous disdain for my kind. He's loathed demons for as long as I can remember, and been at war with us for centuries, yet he has come here to make a deal with me. Fighting the urge to laugh in his face, I watch his eyes flicking left and right. He wouldn't even look at me. Being cautious and thinking things through is definitely more of an angelic trait you could say, yet here we are…

Nostrils flaring, I let him see my eyes change to their amber hue, and hide my smirk when he gulps, but I'm impressed that he doesn't cower or walk away. He must be desperate. I can work with desperate if it means getting what my father didn't manage to obtain a millennium ago.

"So, let me get this straight," I said, crossing my arms over my chest and glaring down my nose at him. "All you want me to do is kill this girl and the Order, who has been a pain in my ass for centuries, will let us deal with our own without interference?" Lifting one eyebrow to show how ridiculous I find his offer, I watch him squirm.

"Yes." Clearing his throat, he squares his shoulders and takes a deep breath. "As I said, the details about it are confidential to the Order and do not need to be discussed. All you need to know is if you kill the girl, we will look the other way unless you or yours get in our way. If that happens, I can't promise we will let it slide."

"Why?" I ask, my eyes narrowing when panic flashes in his eyes.

Catching himself for slipping up and showing emotion, he snarls at me. "Why does it matter to you, demon?" I can't hide the smirk anymore as he continues. "I'm giving you an opportunity no one has ever dared offer and here you are looking a gift horse in the mouth!"

"From where I'm standing, old man, not one of you ever offers anything that doesn't give you the upper hand, least of all to me and mine. So, you'll have to excuse this lowly demon for wanting to know what kind of hole you're trying to make me dig for myself. Now speak! I don't have time for this. I have hunters to hunt and rogues to kill." A menacing smile grows on my face as his eyes widen.

"You don't fool me, Eric! I know a lot more about you than you realize. Take the offer while it's still on the table. I can't promise you it'll still stand if I walk away." He angles his head at me, a stern look plastered on his face.

Okay, the old man has a backbone, and his words ring true to my ears.

"When?" At his confused face, I laugh. "When do you want the girl dead?"

"You'll do it?" There's so much hope in his eyes that uneasiness gnaws at my gut.

Shrugging a shoulder, I say, "What's one more dead hunter to me?"

He squirms again. "Tomorrow! I'll give you the time and place where she'll be. Just leave the rest of her team alone. But you must do it tomorrow!" His words rush out of his mouth, and I hear a trace of fear in them. Does he think I'll change my mind? The disquiet grows inside me.

"You do that and she won't be your problem anymore." I listen intently when he mutters the time and place before I turn and walk away from him.

"Thank you, Eric. You won't regret it!" he calls after me. My feet falter while my cold heart shrivels. *What the fuck have I just agreed to?*

I almost jog to my car. While driving to see the only

MAYA DANIELS

person that might make some sense out of all this, my mind reels. The city blurs around me, and before I know it, I'm walking into the reception area of our place of operations. The pretty brunette behind the desk straightens up and starts batting her lashes like a bitch in heat. I might take her up on her offer eventually, but I don't need complications in my life right now. A shiver runs down my spine at the thought of commitment.

"Eric!" she purrs, leaning on the desk and pushing her boobs up. "How wonderful to see you again." I don't come here often. I don't need to be seen to do my job.

"Lauren, is Maddison here?" I give her one of my trademark smiles. Her eyes dilate and her breathing speeds up.

"Yes," she says in a breathy voice, her eyes roaming the full span of my chest. I smile to myself. *Silly woman doesn't know what she's asking for.* "She just came in."

"Thanks!" Rapping my knuckles on the desk twice, I stride through the doors towards Maddison's office.

I don't knock. Instead, I push the door open and walk inside where my eyes immediately connect with Maddison's blue ones.

"What's wrong?" Her musical voice usually calms me down, but not today.

She listens attentively while I describe meeting the crazy old man. When I'm done, we sit looking at each other for long moments. Lifting her arms, Maddison rubs

12

little circles on her temples. I can relate to that. Ever since I walked away, I've had a raging headache.

"This…" she starts, then shakes her head. "This is either the best day of our very long lives, or it's a setup!"

"I'd go with setup."

"Of course, you would." Twisting her mouth in displeasure, she glowers at me. I lift both eyebrows. "It's worth the try," she tells me gingerly after a while.

"That's what I'm thinking." Tired, I scrub my hands over my face. "I'll go, and if it's a setup, I'll get my ass out of there as soon as possible. If any of them die in the process, oh, well…oops!"

"You're hoping it's a setup." Maddison laughs, and I grin at her.

"Come on, how bad can it be?"

———

The next day, while I'm perched on the roof of a run-down house in a shitty suburb of Atlanta, I realize how bad it can be. Five hunters exit an SUV and spread out. The old man said the blonde is my target. What the asshole didn't say was that she'd take my breath away. A fucking hunter and I can't pick my jaw off the roof when she walks over and sandwiches herself between a horde of rogue demons and her team. Her hair floats around her beautiful face with every move. Her breasts bounce, pulling my eyes down like a siren song, and her narrow waist and round hips sway in sync with them. Belts wrap around her lower body and thighs—thighs that I want wrapped around me. Full lips press firmly together, and green eyes flare with the excitement of the hunt and hatred for the rogues. My heart thumps hard against my breastbone when she pulls out two large revolvers, spinning them in her hands before pointing them at the horde. A breathtaking smile brightens her entire face before she speaks.

"Playtime, motherfuckers!" Her sultry voice caresses my ears, and I know that very moment how fucked I am.

"Fucking old man could've just fucking killed me!" I snarl at the starless sky.

Chapter Three

Helena…

Present Day

Scalding hot water pounds my shoulders as I lean my forearms on the tiles and try to wake up properly. The past week has been one intense hunt after another, and they keep getting more difficult. Even with fast healing, my entire body hurts. The muscles knotted in my back and shoulders feel like tennis balls under my skin.

We've lost so many hunters that it's morbid to walk through the halls of our home thinking, *Say something, it might be the last time you see them.* No one in the sanctuary talks about what is going on, but we all feel the tension building like a ticking bomb with the patrons. The entire Forbearer's ministry has been holed up in the library, only coming out to send us on hunts in groups. The excitement of the chase has gone. No more jokes or slaps on the back while making plans to hang out when we get back. Now, only dull eyes track our movements, like we are going in front of a firing squad. For many, that is precisely the case.

Lifting my face towards the showerhead, I hope the water can wash away the gloomy thoughts clouding my mind. I have the urge to go kick the doors in, storm the library, and demand answers, but after that cursed night, I have secrets to keep. Secrets that might create a bright flashing arrow pointing at my head with the sign *Imposter* and a reason for me to defend my loyalties. Goosebumps cover my entire body and a cold wave of nausea hits at that thought. My team is the only one not to lose a hunter, and it's not because we're better than the rest. The abominations are more interested in getting to me than trying to stay alive. The four people in my group all keep their mouths closed, even though they watch me from the corners of their eyes. There is a new wariness surrounding us.

Loud pounding on the door sounds over the noise of

the water. I turn the shower off, smoothing my hands over my face and hair. The liquid glides down my back, but it's painful instead of soothing. Pulling the screen door open and snatching a towel, I hurry to open the door before whoever it is wakes the entire place up.

"There you are!" Amanda prances inside, pushing past me and acting like she didn't just try to break the door in.

"Are we under attack?" Closing the door, I lean back on it, crossing my hands over my chest.

"No." Grinning, she jumps on my bed, bouncing a few times before she settles. Innocently, she blinks her big eyes at me.

"Why are you here at four AM?" I'm glaring because this is my time, a time when I can think, collect my thoughts, and not worry about anything or anyone.

"I've been waiting for you to let me know when you're ready to talk because I figured you needed time to process what happened." The mask of playfulness is gone. "Since you want to play stupid, I figured I'd invite myself in for a heart to heart."

"I have nothing to talk about!" Snapping at her, I gather my clothes, snatching them as if it's their fault I'm grumpy, and walk towards the bathroom to dress.

"I beg to differ, and I assure you that neither you nor I are going out that door until we talk." Her voice floats to the bathroom where I drop everything on the floor and lean on the sink with my head hanging down.

She has a point. I know it. She knows it, too. The

problem is that I honestly don't know what to tell her. When I look back on that night a week ago, I hope if I ignore it, it will go away." But I must face the music and get to the bottom of it, no matter what *it* is.

"Did you hear what the abomination that raked my arm said?" My voice is low, but I don't need to lift my head to know that Amanda is standing at the door. Her eyes poke at my back like accusing fingers.

"No," she says softly, as if scared to speak louder in case I stop talking.

"Soon, all of you will regret getting involved in things that you know nothing about." Lifting my head, I lock eyes with her in the mirror. "After that, we lost dozens every night, and each night only our team comes back with the same number as when we left. They don't fight or even try to protect themselves. They're too busy trying to get their hands on me. You can't tell me that you haven't noticed."

"Oh, I've noticed!" She nods adamantly. "But you're a hot piece of ass, so you can't blame them for wanting all those yummy curves!" Her eyebrows go as high as her hairline and the ring she has on the side of her left eyebrow sparkles in the light. She sighs and stops the charade when I just watch her deadpan. "Listen, girl, they're demons! Who knows why they say and do half the things they do? Our job is not to exchange pleasantries with them. We're there to kill the suckers and send them back to hell. It's what we've been born to do!" Spreading her hands wide, she looks at me as if expecting applause for the speech.

"What if it was right?" Searching her eyes through the mirror, her forehead furrows. Turning around, I lean on the sink. "What if something has changed that we don't know about? I mean, they've never spoken to us." Frowning, I nibble on my lower lip. "Right? They've never spoken before now?"

"Not that I know of, no." Pursing her lips, it looks painful to admit that fact.

"So, my point is," I say, pointing a finger at her, "why now? And why me?"

"It could've spoken to anyone if it was a Chatty Cathy." Cocking her head, she looks like she is seriously considering her ridiculous statement.

"Amanda, be serious for a second, please. I'm not joking!"

"I know you're not, Hel." Coming closer, she grabs both my hands in hers, squeezing gently. "You are overthinking, as usual. We're the good guys, remember? There's nothing to question or even think twice about." There is so much sincerity in her big eyes that my chest hurts with how much I want to believe everything she says. If only that damn night hadn't happened. "They tell us where the abominations are, we send them back to hell, and everyone is happy and safe. The good guys always win."

"The good will always win," I repeat, and the pressure

in my head and chest lessens. "Thank you! I think it's just the number of deaths this last week that's messing with me. It all just hit out of nowhere." Pulling my hands out of hers, I rub them over my face.

"Yeah, I figured it was something like that. You're always the one that takes our losses the hardest. It's not your job to babysit all of us, and you can't save everyone, my fearless, beautiful friend. I just wish you knew what a great person you are and how much we love you for it." Tugging me to her, she wraps her arms around me, squeezing me tight. "Even George, the jerk!" Snickering, she pulls back to look at my glaring face. "I think being a jerk is his way of flirting with you."

I push her away as she laughs in my face while making kissing sounds. Shaking my head, I can't help but chuckle along with her as I try to place a hand over her mouth to make her stop.

"You're the jerk now! Stop this crap!" Laughing, we wrestle, and she chortles even louder when I almost lose the towel. The pounding on the door has us both sobering up in a second as I rush to open it, clutching the towel to my chest. George stands at the door and looks me up and down slowly before his dark eyes settle on mine.

"We've been summoned to the library. Another team never made it back." His words feel like punches to my chest as I numbly stare at him.

Chapter Four

Twenty-five minutes later, I follow my team through the heavy double doors carved with Holy symbols and intricate crosses to enter the library. The musty smell of old books and parchments calms my thundering heart, which is doing its best to push out of my chest hammering my ribcage as I turn around and pull the doors closed behind me. Reluctantly turning around, my eyes scan everything, marking all corners, shadows, exits, and potential weapons. It's an ingrained reaction I developed in my training through the years, and all my mentors were proud of me for it. At the moment, I'm not so sure they feel the same because three of them narrow their eyes at me when they notice my reaction.

The large room is as big as a public library, but that's where the similarities end. Three walls are lined top to bottom with shelves full of books, one broken by a large window, and a wooden ladder with wheels leans to one side. Between them, a sizable mahogany desk long enough to accommodate twelve people is nestled with high-back chairs around it. Only four are occupied when we enter, and all the occupants are watching us walk towards them like we're the dirt on their shoes.

My boots make clicking sounds as they touch the fishbone wooden floors and the sound echoes around me as if I'm moving inside a tomb. I don't know why I feel this dread rising with each breath I take, but my gut feeling has never failed me to this day. I doubt it'll start now, so I know something terrible is about to happen. The rows and rows of books that go on as far as they eye can see bother me. It makes me feel open and vulnerable when I stop to face the people sitting at the table, which is ridiculous, since the sanctuary is an old monstrosity that used to be a church and it's built on blessed soil. It's not a feeling I've experienced often, at least not that I can remember, anyway.

I'm the last one to stop as we line up shoulder to shoulder and my eyes subconsciously flick to the letter opener that resembles a sword sitting idly on top of the polished desk. That, too, doesn't go unnoticed by the men facing us.

"I'm happy to see you finally decided to grace us with your presence." Samuel, the youngest of the four patrons, stares daggers at each of us in turn. "But I see what the delay was." One of his bushy eyebrows goes up when he settles his mud-brown eyes on me. "Are we all dressed presentable enough to satisfy your liking, Helena?"

I knew that it would eventually come down to this. For some reason, it bothers the patrons greatly that I always style my hair and do my makeup, even before a hunt. Amanda looks like an anime character, and still, I bother them more. Apparently, I have too much potential to waste time on unimportant things. They just don't know what's important to me. All four of them now have their eyes on me, and I see Amanda and Cass fidget out of the corner of my eye. No amount of fidgeting can keep my mouth shut, unfortunately.

"I didn't think it would be appropriate to show up here wet and wrapped in a towel, sir! If I knew it was that urgent, I wouldn't have thought twice about it and would've rushed here just as I was when George knocked on my door at four AM. I didn't think you would feel comfortable with me standing here half naked," I tell them evenly while doing my best not to smirk when their faces start turning red with each word that comes out of my mouth.

"You…you should be set on guard duty for showing such disrespect, young lady!" Samuel stutters, his sagging cheeks flopping around, reminding me of a bulldog. I almost snort at the image.

What the hell is wrong with you! my mind screams at me, but I feel like someone else has taken possession of my body and the words coming out are not my own. Too bad we can't be possessed, so I can't really blame it on that, only on my own stupidity. As I'm arguing in my own head, I see the gloating look that enters Solomon's eyes, and they almost glitter with satisfaction, as if I've given him a reason to keep me from going on a hunt. The dread I was feeling earlier doubles.

"I was told a team didn't return last night. I meant no disrespect, I simply wanted to be ready if we had to leave straight away to search for them." Hurriedly, I try to remedy what my big mouth messed up.

"They were found," Adam says in a hollow voice, cutting off whatever Samuel was about to say.

Silence descends around us, and I look from one patron to the other, waiting to hear more. No one says anything as they stare at us with vacant eyes, not seeing us at all. Absentmindedly, I glide my right hand over my gun, the cold feel of the metal calming the whirlwind of thoughts that are making me dizzy. Something makes me look at Hector, the last patron in the room, and my heart skips a beat as I notice one side of his mouth quirking before he schools his features. *What's going on? Or have I started hallucinating?*

"Did anything unusual happen this past week on your hunts, or with your assigned tasks?" Samuel continues as if they didn't just tell us five of the people we've known our whole lives are dead.

"Who?" Hearing my own voice makes me flinch internally, and I hear the barely-audible groan from both Amanda and Cass. I want to know which team is lost to us, but I get ignored like I haven't spoken at all.

"There were more demons than usual, sir!" George speaks loud and clear in a voice that would make any drill sergeant proud. "It started a week ago to the day, and it increased daily."

"We all know about the increasing numbers, child." Hector speaks for the first time, his voice deep, fatherly, and even. "We are asking about something unusual, something that's never happened before."

While Samuel looks like a bulldog with his floppy cheeks, bald head, and chubby sausage fingers, even when wearing the black robes, Hector is regal and grace incarnate. Slim and tall, his white hair is cut short and it matches his lined face perfectly. His presence alone demands respect and obedience. The other two, Adam and Solomon, are identical twins. Lucky for us, and unlucky for him, Adam has a deep scar cutting his left cheek from under his hairline to under his chin, sitting like a reminder that someone has tried to cut his face off but failed. Though it does help to identify which twin you are looking at. They both have salt and pepper hair cut the same way and brushed to the side, as well as narrow, angular faces with a long, pointed nose sticking above thin lips. Built like jocks, it's not hard to guess they used to be hunters like us at some point in their lives.

My breath freezes in my lungs as I consider that question. To make things worse, the twins are looking at me intently, as if trying to read my mind. I'm sending prayers to Heaven that they can't hear the screaming my brain is doing at the moment. When George clears his throat and appears about to answer, I can't take it anymore.

"One of the demons spoke to me!" Relief for finally hearing it out loud washes over me a second before the realization hits me that it's not my own voice that said that. It was Amanda's, and my head whips towards her while a sharp pain zings through me from my shoulder to the base of my skull from the movement.

"Saying what exactly?" Steepling his sausages, or fingers as others would call them, on the desk, Samuel leans over it, his eyes betraying his excitement. Hector hasn't taken his light blue eyes off my face while I'm gaping at Amanda like a fish out of water.

"Something about regretting getting involved…" Tilting her head, she taps one finger on her lips as if thinking. "I believe. Something along those lines, but I didn't pay much attention."

"A demon spoke and you didn't pay attention?" Adam snaps, almost growling at her through clenched teeth.

"I'm sorry, sir! I was trying to kill it and stay alive. I didn't know I should try to chat it up." Her face dead serious, she blinks those big, brown, innocent eyes at them, looking from one patron to the other. My heart jumps to my throat where it tries to choke me for a second before it drops to my feet. *What on earth is she doing?*

"Did any of the rest of you have something similar happen?" Adam squints at each of us in turn.

"I doubt it." Amanda keeps talking and I fight the urge to slap a hand over her mouth. "No one can hear themselves think, let alone listen if a demon is talking when Helena starts using her girls." Nonchalantly she waves a hand, indicating my guns. "I was away from the group, chasing the abomination, when this happened."

"Out!" Samuel snaps, and I jump a little from the volume in his voice.

They've been angry before, many times. But they've never screamed like now. All of us turn at the same time and start walking towards the doors as fast as our legs can carry us without running for the exit. Jared grabs the doors and pulls them open, and I calm down a little when the fresh air from the hallway hits my face like a breeze.

"Not you, Amanda!" Adam's words feel like they hit me at the back of my knees and I stagger, bumping into George's back. "You stay! They can go."

Pushing myself off George, I turn around to walk back

inside, but both he and Jared grab hold of my arms, while Cass grabs the multiple belts I like to wear around my hips like she's trying to reign in a horse. Amanda winks before pushing the doors closed in my face. All the adrenaline that was making me crazy inside the library leaves me at once, and my eyes roll to the back of my head while my body crumbles to meet the floor.

Chapter Five

Gasping for air, I flail my arms, trying to grab hold of something substantial to anchor me to reality. My chest hurts as if my ribcage is ready to burst through my skin, and my eyes snap open when my upper body jerks me into a sitting position. Sucking in short, sharp breaths, I look around, not recognizing where I am. Everything is gray, including the closed door that I'm eyeing so I can bolt out of here.

"Easy there, Hel! Breathe!" Jared's smooth voice makes my head jerk in his direction, my hair flying around my face. "Breathe," he repeats, his blue eyes calm and steady on my face. He's sitting on the chair next to the bed that I'm apparently occupying.

Unable to answer him from lack of oxygen, I stare at him wide-eyed and he starts taking deliberate slow, deep breaths, as if trying to teach me how to breathe. Subconsciously, I follow his directions, and after a few moments, I finally feel enough air enter my sore lungs.

"That's it! Keep breathing slow and even." His voice is soothing, and I nod jerkily, following directions until I feel the muscles of my body unlock from the state they were in.

"Amanda!" Still gasping, I manage to utter my friend's name, searching his eyes.

"She's fine. They're downstairs getting instructions for our hunt tonight. I was told I should stay here to look after you until they come back." With a sheepish smile, he rubs the back of his neck. "It's Amanda we're talking about. She's always fine." Awkwardly chuckling, his boyish face relaxes me even more.

"It wasn't her." The words hurt my throat, but I have the urge to say them out loud. "You know it wasn't her that the abomination spoke to, right? It was me!"

"Yeah…" Still rubbing his neck, Jared won't meet my eyes. "We know. But we can talk about that later when the others come. They'll tell you better what we think the deal is. You know me, I'd rather just tag along and let you guys do the talking."

"Where are we?" Looking around so as not to make him more uncomfortable than he already is, I try to see if there is anything that's not gray in this room.

"My room." Clearing his throat, he fidgets. "I never had the urge to decorate it much." His words sound like an apology and I take a breath to answer him, but his next words feel like a knife in my heart. "I never thought I'd stay alive long enough to matter, you know? Then, I got assigned to your team, and, well, here we are." He looks around as if seeing the room for the first time as well. "I just never changed it." With a frown, his blue eyes lock on my green ones.

"Who cares about a room, Jared? You don't have to do anything you don't like doing." Letting him see that I mean every word, I don't look away. "And you'll live for a very long time if I have anything to say about it." A look of shocked surprise makes him jerk upright. "It's a promise!"

"Thank you!" His eyes glitter like he's fighting tears. "I'm not the best hunter, Hel, I know that. I never wanted to be a hunter to start with. Unlike you. The rest are all good, but you're still better."

"I'm just like the rest, Jared. Well, just like the rest plus the guns." I grin at him, making him chuckle.

"Yeah, right! We all know they're planning on putting you with the Elite hunter teams. We just hope we'll get to stay with you." He groans as soon as his words are spoken, placing a hand over his forehead as if in pain.

"What did you just say?" He's still groaning as if in pain, but the cat is out of the bag already. "Jared! Look at me, damn it! How do you know about that? Who told you? And why didn't anyone tell me?" I know I'm asking a million questions at once, but I'm so shocked I can't stop talking.

"Let's just wait for the others, please? They'll tell you everything," Jared pleads with words and with his eyes.

As if on cue, the door opens and Amanda, Cass, and George walk in, their faces solemn, but smiles appear when they see me sitting up on the bed. Staring at them with what I assume is a confused and shocked look on my face, it takes a moment for them to register the tension and panic in the room. Cass hurries to Jared and sits on his lap, wrapping her arms around him while pulling his head to her chest. They are such an unusual couple. Jared with his tall and lean physique, blond hair, and a blue-eyed boy-next-door look, while Cass is short and curvy with caramel skin, dark chocolate eyes, and thick, curly hair falling around her shoulders. I start when Amanda grabs hold of my hand, my head jerks away from the two cuddling on the chair. George stands next to the bed, looking down at me with those dark, fathomless eyes, his brown hair flopping over his forehead and covering his frown.

"What's wrong? Are you okay?" Amanda tugs on my hand to get my attention.

"I'm fine!" I watch her eyebrows go up and I groan at my snappish reply. Taking a deep breath, I go on, "I mean, I'm fine. Everything just piled up, and the anxiety made me lightheaded…I think. Which reminds me!" Pulling her so Amanda can fully turn towards me, I grab both her hands in mine. "What happened? What did they say, and most important, why on earth did you say it was you? What possessed you to lie?"

"Calm down, Hel!" I growl angrily at her while she's trying to placate me. "Okay, fine!" She huffs. "I lied because you suck at it, okay?"

"What?" Taken aback by the comment, confusion makes me shake my head. "What's that supposed to mean?"

"It means something is not right and no one is saying a word until we know what it is!" George snaps, speaking for the first time. I scowl at him, but he's unfazed. "As much as I love seeing those green eyes shoot death daggers at me, it's got nothing to do with you! Well…" He tilts his head left and right as if debating it, making his hair flip around. "I'm not sure it has nothing to do with you, but that's not the most important thing. Amanda's right. You suck at lying. Even if it's omitting the truth, it'll be written all over your face. So, Amanda taking it upon herself to cover for you was the smart thing to do."

"I told you *jerk* is his flirting mode." Amanda bumps her shoulder on mine and the couple on the chair snicker at that. I ignore her.

"What does that mean? Are we talking about the demon?" Looking from one face to the next, I'm trying to figure out what they're telling me.

"No. We're talking about sending a team of hunters on

a mission that was clearly above our level and obviously for an Elite team." George apparently took it upon himself to be the voice for the team, so, I just stare at him, waiting to hear the rest. "We shouldn't have been there last week. We're good, yes!" His chest puffs up with pride. "But we're not that good. You might be better than the rest of us, but unless they wanted you dead, no one in their right mind would've sent you there with just us watching your back."

"What are you saying, George?" I search his eyes as my body grows numb and a nauseating feeling makes cold sweat break out all over me. "What are you telling me?"

"Someone wanted either you or us out of the way. There's no other explanation. The fact that we came back without a scratch…" He pulls a face at that, looking pointedly at my forearm, and as if called, the now-smooth skin there, throbs at his words. "It was either good luck, or else we just painted a larger target on our backs."

"Why the hell would anyone here want to harm us? Are you all insane?" Incredulously, I turn my head, searching their faces for something to tell me that this is some sick joke. These people here are our family. They've raised us, trained us. It's the only home we know. But, instead of laughing and telling me 'Gotcha!' like they usually would, only solemn faces stare at me. George holds my stare the longest, and without a word, lifts his hand towards me, handing me an envelope.

Chapter Six

"We're not going!" Throwing the paper at George's chest, I stare down my nose at him as if he's the one responsible for this stupidity.

"I don't think we have a choice, Hel." My narrowed gaze turns to Amanda, but she just presses her purple-painted lips into a thin line. "Glare all you want! What are you going to do, huh? Walk down there and ask the patrons 'Which one of you is trying to kill me? I'm not going anywhere.'" She mimics my husky voice, and I really want to strangle her.

"They're talking about a nest of hundreds!" Looking around at all of them, my stomach feels like it'll empty itself at any moment. "Hundreds! None of us are coming back alive. You understand that, right?"

"We have our secrets, too!" Jared quips and shrinks in the chair when we all turn to look at him.

"What aren't you telling me?" Suspicion eats at me and I hate it. This whole thing feels like a nightmare I really want to wake up from.

"We've been collecting weapons, healing salves, money, you name it, this last week." My eyebrows hit my hairline when I look at Amanda, but she just rolls her eyes at me. "You were too busy avoiding us, remember?"

"I thought something was wrong with me." Feeling warmth on my cheeks at my own stupidity, I press the backs of my hands against them to cool them down. My white skin doesn't help hide my embarrassment. "I thought it'd make you doubt my loyalties."

"Things can make me doubt your sanity, Hel. Never your loyalty." Amanda snickers at her own joke, but I don't laugh. "What?" Wide-eyed, she spreads her arms. "Not funny?" Cocking her head to the side, she blinks few times. "Not even a little funny?"

"This is insane!" Grabbing my hair in both hands, I just stare at them. "Maybe the elite teams are busy. There must be a logical explanation for this. It's been getting crazier by the day, after all. And we are really good at what we do. So…" Dragging out the word, I try to reason with them. "They're sending us! I mean, Hector is sending *me* there! Hello! We're talking about the same man that would trample over anyone in his way to catch me if I tripped so I wouldn't have a scratch on me."

That's another thing. Hector, the oldest patron we have, is my father. Well, not biological, but he took me in when I was a few days old, and he's the only father I've ever known. Is he the best parent? I don't know. Is he the worst? I couldn't say, since I've never had a different one. I am happy, that much I know. He is strict and has some archaic beliefs, but regardless of that, he has taught me everything I know, starting with what is right and wrong and going all the way to hair products and makeup. Whenever I ask about my real parents, he only pats my head, telling me an archangel brought me to his door. Snorting, I always roll my eyes at his joke, especially since he calls me 'little angel.' With my large breasts and round hips, I most definitely could be related to the chubby cupid.

"That's what's messing with my head as well." George pulls me from my trip down memory lane. "If it were just the rest of us, I would've been getting in their faces, asking which one is possessed. But if there's one thing I'm sure of, it's that Hector would not let a hair go missing from your head—and he just sat there, calmly, when they gave me this!" He waves the paper with the coordinates in the air, wrinkling his nose at it.

It looks comical to see George, with his broad

shoulders and arms as big as my thighs, sneer at a piece of paper like it'll bite him. He was never fond of books or reading, not even at school, so seeing him like this makes me snort before I try to cough and cover it up.

"What?" he snaps at me, and I can't help it, I laugh. The others join, too. Shaking his head, he lowers the paper, and after a moment, he chuckles as well. "What a fucking mess." He rubs a hand over his square jaw and face.

"We'll be fine. I'm actually thinking that we might even be like a cleanup team. Maybe we're just cleaning up what's left of it." Cass speaks for the first time while she's still cuddling Jared.

"Yeah. I wouldn't go that far, but as I said, I think Hector would be screaming bloody murder if it was really as bad as it looks on paper," I assure them, more confident by the minute that I'm right. "I'd also like to know who told you guys that I might be pulled to an elite team? Because I have a team, thank you very much. I don't need, or want, a new one."

"For someone who likes to be quiet, my friend, you talk too much!" Amanda glares at Jared, and the poor guy would merge with the chair if he could. "It's been a rumor for a few months now, Hel. Ever since that guy, what's his name?" She snaps her fingers around, waiting for someone to supply the name. "Aha! Benjamin. Thank you, Amanda!" She gives herself a high five. "Ever since big old Ben never came back from a mission, they've been looking for a replacement. Out of all the teams, so far, you have the most kills in hunts. Plus, miss goody-two-shoes, you follow orders, and everyone knows that you are the favorite. It's a logical assumption."

A knock on the door stops further questioning or arguments and Jared stands up while Cass scrambles to get off his lap. He looks at us in turn before squaring his shoulders, walking to the door, and yanking it open. I almost expect him to punch whoever it is on the other side.

"Ah, good! All of you are here." Adam walks in, making Jared take a few involuntary steps back so they don't bump chest to chest. "Are we ready, then?" He looks at us with his eyebrows raised, and it's pulling the skin on his face weirdly, making his scar more visible.

"Ready for what?" I ask dumbly, unable to stop staring at the black long-sleeved shirt and black cargo pants that he's wearing instead of his usual robes.

"To go clean up the nest of abominations!" he tells me excitedly as his eyes glitter with excitement. "I'm going with you!" A large smile stretches his lips and he claps his hands, rubbing them together.

Amanda and I both jump a little at the clapping sound, making him chuckle. Without waiting for us to say anything, he steps out the same way he came in. We all look at one another, the absurdity of the whole thing not lost on us. Sliding my hands over my hair, I take a deep breath, exhaling it slowly. We will be okay, I'm sure.

"Go on, get out, go home." Mumbling, I watch my team. They nod in understanding as we turn towards the door.

"Hurry along, then! There's no time to waste!" Adam yells from down the hall.

Chapter Seven

Leaning on the back of the black SUV that brought us here, chewing on my thumbnail, I scan the surrounding area. Another suburb that must've been a joy to live in not long ago stares back at me. The cookie-cutter homes that must have been idyllic are replaced with broken fences, yellowed grass lawns, and discarded broken furniture and toys that feel like accusing fingers in my face, and there's not one human in sight, dead or otherwise. I almost feel the ground under my boots screaming at me, "You're too late! Where were you when they needed you?"

It's a dead end. That's where the patrons sent us, with instructions to clean up a demon's nest. There might have been hundreds, or even thousands of them here, but as it stands now, there is not even one left that I can take my confusion and frustration out on. Everyone else is walking in and out of the homes and buildings, looking for a sign —or anything really—that might point us in the right direction. It's impossible for an entire neighborhood to just vanish, leaving only inanimate objects behind. It looks like an abandoned town after the Apocalypse. The wind picks up, whistling eerily among the sparse trees, adding to the dread I feel.

"Anything?" I call out to Jared when he walks out of yet another gloomy, broken home, but he just shakes his head sadly and strides towards another yard. "Run along, then. I'll just sit right here…doing nothing!" I mumble under my breath as I watch him disappear through yet another door.

I guess this is my punishment for having a mouth I can't control. Adam made sure I stand here in case something shows up while they're searching. Guard duty, my ass. This feels like torture as I keep on abusing my thumb with my teeth and tap the fingers of my other hand on the buckles of my belts. He knows how much I want to do something, if only to keep from sitting idly. But that's why I'm here and all of them are searching.

A shadow darkens the side of the closest home before it blends in with the rest. My body stiffens, but I watch it from the corner of my eyes while my hand glides smoothly along the belts around my hip until I get a good grip on my gun. The bullets I use are infused with holy water and salt. Made out of blessed metal, they kill the abominations like nothing else I've ever used. The guns were Hector's gift to me for my eighteenth birthday, and I haven't had them out of arms' reach since that day. Longer than the usual revolver, they almost look like something you would see on a safari hunt, which is not far from what I'm doing. The difference is that I love animals and would never hurt one. Abominations, on the other hand, are fair game.

Another shadow, this one on the opposite side of the road, darkens, expands, and retracts within the blink of an eye but just long enough for me to notice it. I'm not sure if it's the adrenaline pumping through me at the prospect of a hunt, or it's an unusual fact that everyone is still holed up somewhere and I haven't seen them exit for a tad too long. Placing my bent fingers at my lips, I whistle gently, hoping I don't startle whoever it is that's sneaking up on us. Seeing Amanda walk out the door a few houses down from the SUV calms the unease that I am feeling, but it's short-lived as panic grips me again, making me unable to warn her.

Lifting her head up, her face illuminated by the yellow light of the street lamp, she looks at me with a broad smile a second before my heart lodges in my throat. The most massive demon I have ever seen in my life, his skin as black as night and eyes as bright yellow as the sun, looms behind her, towering over her a moment before I see its sharp teeth flash in the light, then sink into her neck. Amanda's face, frozen in shock, is the last thing seared into my brain before the demon slinks back in the shadows and I can't see it anymore. All hell breaks loose in a split second.

They come out from everywhere. I have no clue how many there are; it could be a handful or hundreds. All I know is I need to get to Amanda. One gun in each hand, I sprint forward, firing at anything that moves around me. The gunshots have this quiet neighborhood singing a song of death and destruction, and demons drop like flies everywhere I look. More replace the ones that have fallen, and it feels like I'm slowly running in place instead of sprinting because I must stop and turn in circles so they don't close in on me from my back.

Movement makes me hesitate when someone slinks behind me, but a demon screams and drops on the ground, which means one of my team has my back. Ignoring whoever it is, I continue to press on so I can get to Amanda. Like a well-oiled machine, we make progress, leaving abominations the likes of which I've never seen before in our wake. When I reach the place where she last stood, I wish that I never lived long enough to get to her. She always looked like a doll, so perfectly beautiful and porcelain-like. At the moment, in front of me on the ground, she looks like a broken one. Her beautiful brown eyes stare unseeing, while her head rests at an odd angle and her body is crumpled in a heap on the ground. A pool of blood surrounds her, looking like a black puddle in the night.

My hands drop to my sides as I stand numbly, staring at my best friend. Grunts and thuds sound all around. But the demons can take me for all I care in that moment. I didn't make it to her on time. The shock is so sharp I can't even cry, even though my soul screams inside me. All I can do is stand and stare unblinkingly at her.

"You better snap out of it, cupcake! I can't hold them back on my own. You can grieve later when we get out of here." A deep baritone reaches my ears, and the effect on me is like a punch in my chest. The air whooshes out of my lungs as my head snaps in his direction.

The most stunning and intriguing man I have ever seen in my life is the one that has been guarding my back. His dark brown hair is held away from his face in a small ponytail, but the fringe has slipped from the band and falls over one side, making me want to reach up and tuck it behind his ear. Smooth, tan skin stretches over high cheekbones and a perfectly straight nose, while his full, kissable lips spread into a smile. His green eyes sparkle as he winks, while I just gape at him before he spins around and continues to fight the demons. And no, he isn't killing them with a weapon. Only his hands are used as he physically fights them like they are humans.

Panic grips me that he'll get killed until his movements register in my brain. Muscles jump and twist under his tight black t-shirt and jeans as he moves his body in a beautiful, elegant dance of flips, twists, and turns, dropping abominations with each movement. All the while, he maintains a clear circle around us, keeping me safe. A sleeve of tattoos covers his right arm, but there's not enough light to see them properly. No one else is around from my team and there is no sign of Adam. He must be some new hunter from an elite team. Just as I am about to ask if he has seen the others, his movements place him between me and the light. His fist connects with the last standing demon's head, sending it spinning and dropping to the ground, and for a split second I see him clearly. His eyes flash amber, making cold shivers pass through my body from head to toes.

"What the fuck are you?" My mind spins. In shock from losing Amanda and not seeing anyone else, I point my trembling gun at his face.

Chapter Eight

"So much gratitude for helping you, cupcake." Huffing, he ignores the gun barrel staring him in the face and smooths his hair away from his forehead with both hands. His biceps bunch up the sleeves of his shirt, pulling my eyes to trace them instead of paying attention to him.

"Stop moving or I will shoot you in the face! I asked, 'what are you?'" My hand gets steadier the longer he keeps that smile on his stupidly handsome face.

"What I am is a long story, too long for it to be told here. The rogues are not all dead, and more will come. I suggest we get out of here before that happens." Dropping the smile, he starts to turn as if expecting me to just follow him because he told me to.

The sound of the gun going off echoes in the now eerily silent street, like a bomb has exploded a second before his knees buckle and he drops to all fours on the ground. I expect him to scream, maybe even die, although killing him isn't my ultimate goal. What I don't expect is for him to just grunt as if he is lifting something heavy, reach behind to the back of his left thigh, and dig out the bullet that is burning his skin with two claw-tipped fingers that morph back to normal as soon as they are out of his wound. My gun lowers slightly as my jaw hits my chest, my wide eyes gaping at him in wonder. My ears buzz so loud I can't hear a thing, and my heart jackhammers in my chest as I watch him lift himself from the ground, standing proud and tall, his shoulders thrown back in an elegant pose. He doesn't even turn to look at me. Just his head turns to the side so I can see his perfect profile, which sends a zing to my lower belly and makes me shift on my feet uncomfortably.

"I see it won't be easy to make you see you don't belong here. Next time you find yourself in a similar situation, I'll be there to guard your back again. You have the choice to come with me if you want to stay alive. If you decide to stay with your *friends* the third time you're in a similar situation, I will not be there to make sure you live. Think about that, cupcake. I'll see you around!" Nodding his head once, he slinks back into the shadows so fast it takes a moment for my brain to decide to kick into gear.

"Hey! Wait!" Rushing towards the house where I last saw the darkening of a shadow, I find nothing. "Come back, you coward!"

A deep, husky chuckle makes the hairs on my neck stand up straight and goosebumps cover my entire body. I spin around like a crazy woman, but there's no one there. Hair flying around my face, chest heaving, and with a death grip on my guns, I keep twirling in a circle, my eyes searching for something, any kind of movement. Anger boils my blood at his mocking chuckle, and lifting both arms, I fire at everything around me, spinning in place. One of these bullets will find him if my eyes can't. When only a *click, click* can be heard and no more bullets are left, an ear-piercing whistle splits the suddenly quiet street.

"Helena! Stop shooting! You'll kill us all!" Adam's voice echoes somewhere from my right and panting like I just finished running a marathon, I turn towards it.

"Where were you?" Snapping at him, I watch as he moves towards me from down the street. "Where are the others?"

"I was hoping you'd tell me." Frowning, he slows down, his confused gaze searching the area around us. "You're the first one I saw."

"They were with you! Searching!" I snap, uneasiness

making me want to scream at him and shake him to tell me where my team is.

"So? They'll come out, just like I did. Need I remind you who is in charge of this mission?" Disapproval is clearly written all over Adam's face, but I couldn't care less.

"Where were you when she needed you?" All the emotions I'd been suppressing from the moment I saw Amanda up until this second collide in me and I scream at Adam's face, flinging my hand towards my best friend's body. He only frowns. "Don't you even care that she's dead?"

"Who's dead?" His eyes flick from somewhere behind me to my eyes. "Helena, are you feeling okay?"

Painfully slow and dreading every second, I turn to look behind me where I know Amanda's lifeless body lays crumpled in a heap on the ground. What I find instead is the empty yard of a broken home. Confusion, fear, and dare I say hope swirl in me, making me feel lightheaded. Maybe I imagined it all and she's still alive. The bodies of the demons would be long gone regardless. It takes half a minute to a minute for them to disintegrate into shadows after they're sent back to hell. The tiny sliver of hope gets squashed like a bug when I see the pool of blood still spreading on the ground where Amanda's body used to be.

"She's gone, but you can check the blood. It'll confirm it was her. The demon killed her. I didn't get to her in time." My voice breaks and sounds hollow to my own ears.

"Demon? What are you talking about! We wasted time here in this dead suburb while other places may need our help! Stop playing games and let's get the others." He puts his back to me as he starts to move away just as I notice the other three from my team coming to meet us.

"You find anything?" Adam asks them, but none of them are looking at him. Their eyes are on me as they come to stand where we are.

In a monotone voice, I tell them, "Amanda is dead."

Cass gasps, grabbing her mouth with both hands, and Jared catches her in a tight embrace, pressing her head to his chest. George takes a few long strides and grabs my shoulders, staring at my eyes like he is searching for something.

"Stop with the nonsense this instant!" Adam snaps, but we all ignore him.

"Are you okay?" George asks softly, but I just press my lips together and shake my head jerkily. No, I'm not okay at all.

Clenching his jaw, he pulls me to his chest, wrapping his arms around me. Sobs rack my frame and I feel him press his face against my hair while his body shakes from my tremors. Cass is weeping, while Jared's voice is breaking as he tries to soothe her. In the middle of it all, Adam keeps snapping about me hallucinating, or fear finally getting to me, telling me I'm imagining things that never actually happened. We all stop and stand frozen when a menacing growl rumbles around us. Separating, we press our backs against each other, forming a circle.

"Where did it come from?" Adam's voice comes from somewhere behind me, but I'm not paying attention to him. What has my full attention is the shadow in the form of a sculpted man separating itself from the corner of the house I'm facing. Amber eyes flash for a second, just long enough to wink at me before it again blends into the darkness and disappears.

"Maybe we should spread out. They might finally show up!" Adam says excitedly.

"No one is showing up!" Straightening, I face my team. "We should go back to the Sanctuary."

"And how do you know?" Adam barks at me, his face turning red in anger.

Looking over my shoulder, I search the shadows for a second, but I don't see him again. I can feel him watching though, and I want to get out of here. "I just know."

Chapter Nine

The library is full of people. Most of them I know, but there are a few I've never seen before. This situation is something I've heard about but never experienced, because my team has always been dispatched and returned with the same number of hunters. I've never been behind closed doors when a team loses a member. That's not the case tonight. Tonight, one is missing, and I feel like I'm not even present in the vast room, although, my body is here, standing amid the chaos. The sounds seem muted, like I'm hearing them from underwater, the masses only blurred shapes that angrily flail their arms. Everyone is shouting, and accusing fingers are pointed left and right as if that will somehow magickly bring my best friend back. Not one of them says her name. All I can hear is "The hunter is missing," or "The hunter is dead."

"She has a name." Although I know my words are barely spoken above a whisper, they sound like a scream inside my head.

The shouting continues. No one is paying attention to how broken I feel or how my teammates are dealing with the loss of their friend. The three of them stand mutely around me as well, lost in their own pain and thoughts. We're not important at the moment. From what few words penetrate my barely-functioning brain, the most important thing is that we have one less hunter. I hear something about things changing and the tides turning, but nothing makes sense to me right now. A human being died tonight. A young life full of hopes and dreams is no more because she has fought the good fight, doing the right thing and trying to protect those that can't protect themselves. Does that not deserve a moment of quiet to acknowledge her and mourn this loss before new goals or plans are brought to the forefront of everyone's minds? Something keeps building inside my chest, and it presses on my ribs painfully, making my entire body tremble where I stand.

"She has a name!" My voice booms with so much strength that all the noise stops, and you can hear a pin drop. It's almost as if no one is even breathing. "She has a name," I repeat calmly, my vision finally clearing as I turn my head, looking at all the faces around me. "Was she not worthy enough to be called by her name?" My searching eyes lock with Hector's blue ones where he stands behind that stupid table, leaning on it, his hands clenched into fists. "Amanda! Say it!"

"Ah! You must be Helena!" It's not Hector that speaks, and my eyes snap to his right where a very tall, handsome man I've never seen before stands with his arms crossed. *When the hell did he get here?* I think to myself. "You were right, Hector." Dismissing me, he turns his head towards my father.

"Excuse you?" Glaring at him, I clench my fists at my sides so I don't grab my guns and shoot the asshole.

"She's full of fire. I should've come to see for myself long before today." The asshole keeps talking like I haven't spoken.

"Helena!" Hector's voice is full of warning, and he hasn't taken his eyes off me. He looks like he is about to have a panic attack.

"Who the fuck is this guy?" Seething as I address my father, I fling a hand towards the asshole. "And why won't you at least say her name? For all intents and purposes, she was your daughter as much as I am!"

"Language!" the asshole barks, glowering at me with a look of disapproval on his face. "She…" Taking a calming breath and composing himself, he clears his throat. "Amanda wasn't the first, and she certainly won't be the last hunter we lose. You should celebrate the life she had and honor her courage because she died fighting for what she knew was right. She gave her life to keep evil at bay. She did the right thing!"

I can feel everyone in the library holding their breath. I have no idea who this asshole thinks he is, but he is staring at me so intently I can almost feel his gaze trying to pierce my brain. His blond hair is perfectly combed and styled, slicked away from his face, and light blue eyes that almost look like glass stare at me, unblinking, framed in long, thick lashes that I want to reach up and pluck off one by one as my anger builds inside me. Massive arms are crossed over a large, defined chest with a tight black shirt stretched over it. He is maybe a head taller than Hector, towering over the table that hits the middle of his tree trunk thighs, which are wrapped in black cargo pants. The dark clothing only emphasizes his sculpted *golden boy* appearance. Porcelain skin is stretched over a perfect face that would've taken my breath away if he didn't have that angry grimace on it, or maybe if he'd keep his mouth shut.

"She would not have died if we'd been given the right information on where we were going!" Taking an unconscious step towards him, I scoff, watching him with disdain right back. Someone—and by the tight grip I'm assuming it's George—grabs my arm, but I yank it from his grasp, not looking away from the target of my anger. "Many would've still been alive if we'd known exactly what the fuck was going on instead of having a piece of paper with nothing but coordinates on it, and a vague direction that it could be a large nest and to stay alert. You think you're doing any of us any favors by keeping your doors closed while you're hiding shit? Look where that has gotten us so far!" I'm so angry that I felt like I might start breathing fire any second. The asshole looks so excited at my anger his eyes practically sparkle with it. "And who the hell are you to tell me why she died?"

"Michael, she doesn't know. She doesn't understand —" Hector jabbers, as if trying to excuse my actions, but the asshole lifts a hand in his face, shutting him up mid-sentence. He still hasn't taken his eyes off me.

We stand for a few long moments, staring at each other, neither one willing to back down. Slowly, his narrowed gaze turns into something I can't name, and alarms blare in my head, loud enough that my hands instinctively go to my guns. At my reaction, his bow-shaped lips, the lower fuller than the upper, twitch in a suppressed smile. A shimmering glow sparkles around him, and my entire life turns upside down when two massive wings burst out of his back, making a few people, including Hector, stumble out of his way. My jaw drops to the floor as I watch him wide-eyed, and that finally makes his smile stretch his lips in a very arrogant way. There is no warmth in it, not anymore.

"Hello, Helena. I'm Archangel Michael. Pleased to make your acquaintance."

Chapter Ten

The gasps, the people dropping to their knees, while others groan as if in pain, tells me I'm not the only one in here who thinks when the patrons speak of the Archangels, they mean it figuratively. Apparently, not all of us are aware that the Archangels actually come here to talk with the Forefathers of our organization. From the corner of my eye, I see Hector grab his forehead with his hand, his chin dropping to his chest while I'm still looking dumbfounded at the Archangel, who ruffles the feathers of his wings like a peacock trying to attract a mate.

"Does this mean you can do something to bring

Amanda back?" I hear myself asking, although a million other questions are wreaking chaos in my head.

"No," Michael merely says, still not looking away from me, as if he is waiting for me to do something.

"Then what good are you to us here?" The gasps that echo around me sound outraged, but I really don't give a damn. "Unless you can give us the information we need or bring back those we care about who died—doing *your* bidding, need I remind you—what good are you to us? Or should I have fainted out of excitement for seeing you in all your golden glory? Why aren't you there with us, fighting for, as you say, what is right?" Crossing my arms over my chest so he doesn't see my hands trembling, I square off with him. I might not have wings and I'm only up to his chest if I stand next to him, but I have more attitude than he has ego.

"There are many battles, Helena. Most are worse than what all of you are dealing with here. Those battles are the ones you don't see." He is trying to sound comforting, but what he says sounds so patronizing that my anger from earlier spikes again.

"I don't give a fuck about what I don't see, oh Holy Greatness!" Snapping at him, sarcasm dripping from each word, I come full circle back to my anger. "What I do see, however, is you thinking we're expendable. One more nameless-to-you hunter is gone. Big fucking deal! There are a lot more idiots where that one came from."

"Hel, please stop. This is not the way," Cass mumbles, grabbing my hand and holding onto it like it's her lifeline. I turn my head to look at her while I'm panting with the effort to not start screaming from the top of my lungs. Her dark eyes are red and puffy from crying, all the while still shimmering with unshed tears. "This won't bring her back. I know you're hurting, and I am too, but this…" She looks around, and I follow her gaze, seeing everyone around us staring at me with mixed emotions written on their faces. "This isn't doing any good. Please!"

"Helena, that is enough! Not one more word from you!" Hector's voice startles me and my head snaps in his direction. He's never screamed at me like this in my life. The shock of it renders me speechless as I gape at him. "Am I clear?" His eyes are hard as they stare at me. Mutely and ever so slowly, I nod my head a few times. Turning away from me, his eyes are the last thing to move away after his entire body turns towards the Archangel. He takes a deep breath, composing himself. "I apologize for her behavior; she was raised better. She's hurting badly. She and Amanda grew up together. They were almost like siblings."

The Archangel hasn't taken his eyes off me the entire time. Ignoring my father, his arms drop to his sides and he whirls around, rounding the table and simultaneously slapping Hector in the face with his wing. Hector flinches but only closes his eyes as if pained, his nostrils flaring just enough to know he's irritated. A muscle ticks in his jaw as he clenches his teeth and presses his mouth into a thin line. I would've missed it if I weren't frozen in place by the angel's behavior, still glowering at my father.

Pinpricks cover my body a moment before the angel's shadow announces his nearness to me. Grinding my teeth so I don't flinch away from him, I clench my fists and spin towards him instead. The closer he gets—and he is sauntering as if that will intimidate me more—the more my head raises, maintaining eye contact until my chin is almost pointing at the ceiling. I can feel the heat radiating from his body, and it feels so deceptively comforting, just like the warmth of the sun on a chilly day. It's deceptive because it contradicts the cold look in his eyes that are locked on mine.

"You want to know what has changed, Helena?" His smooth, masculine voice washes over me when he stops so close our bodies are almost touching, and I suppress a shiver as my eyes narrow at him. "You are immune to my charms, I see." Chuckling, his eyes finally have emotion, and it looks like intrigue.

That's so not good for me! my mind screams like a frightened rabbit in front of a wolf.

"I'm immune to everyone's charms, so don't feel special." Blinking a few times, I almost high-five myself at how calm I sound. *Not to that green-eyed monster's charm, you weren't!* my mind supplies and my stomach flipflops at the thought *Fake it till you make it! I can do this!* Cheering myself on in my head, I hold Michael's stare.

Looking down at me, his eyes search mine for something. I silently pray to whoever listens—and hopefully whoever that is, it's not Archangel Michael—that he doesn't find it. I don't know why, but something in me gloats at the idea that the arrogant Archangel can't figure me out. Maybe seeing my best friend die has finally made me lose my mind. This is the good guy, the one that has been protecting humankind from evil since the beginning of time. I have no other explanation for why I feel so strongly about irking him.

"Interesting," he muses while his eyes trace my face, eventually settling on my thinly-pressed lips. Locking eyes with me again, his crinkle at the corners and something inside tells me I'll regret not keeping my mouth shut tonight. "As I was saying, the thing that has changed is that the portal to Hell was recently opened."

The sharp, collective intake of breath feels like it sucks every bit of oxygen from the room. My GPS for evil starts tingling in the pit of my stomach, but for the first time, I ignore it because I'm inside the sanctuary. The damn thing must be broken if it can suddenly sense evil here in the presence of an Archangel.

"What? How? When? Why didn't you say anything sooner?" The patrons all start yelling questions at him, but the angel keeps his eyes locked on mine.

"Apparently the demons figured out that using the

blood of a special kind of angel is the key," Michael speaks, quieting everyone. "You wouldn't know how they got their hands on the blood of an angel, would you, Helena?" Like his words invited it, the throbbing in my arm where the demon scratched me returned tenfold, and it takes everything in me not to cry out in pain.

"How would I know?" Unblinking, I stare back while my mind is replaying Amanda and George's words after we were summoned by the patrons. Amanda took the blame to keep me safe until we figure out what is going on. The least I can do is finish what she started, so I show no emotion.

"What is the meaning of this?" Hector's voice echoes so loud that Michael finally looks away from me to glare at my father. "How dare anyone question her loyalty! That is my child, blood or not!" His words warm me from the inside out, but that ends the moment Michael narrows his eyes at me.

"How indeed," the angel mumbles.

"Excuse me?" I take a step back as if he slapped me. Hector screams something about the Archangel losing his mind and about leaving the Forefather's council, but I tune him out. "Who in their right mind could ever think I would do anything to harm the people inside these walls, or what the Sanctuary stands for?"

After staring at me for I don't know how long, the Archangel says one word, and everyone springs into action until it's as quiet as a tomb in the library.

"Out!"

Now, it's just me, Hector, and him in the vast space. My guilt hangs heavy around me, almost as if a fourth person were here with us.

Chapter Eleven

As soon as the doors are shut, Hector storms towards the angel, seething. I almost expect him to punch Michael in the face but he doesn't. "Whatever it is that you think you know, I can guarantee you it's false! She might be headstrong and speak before she thinks, but that girl has bled for this order more than anyone else can say. So, before you point a finger at her, think really hard, Michael!"

"She knows, then?" One perfectly shaped eyebrow goes up as Michael crosses his arms over his chest, watching my father like he's an annoying fly.

"No, she doesn't." All the anger drains from Hector as

he flicks his eyes towards me, but he doesn't meet my eyes. Uneasiness swirls in my chest.

"What don't I know?" Looking from one to the other, I almost feel dizzy from everything that happened tonight. "And just so we're clear, I've never seen an angel in my life until tonight. I thought you were kinda like a figure of speech. Not actually a living, breathing person." I wave my hand, encompassing his "person" to drive the point home.

At my words, both of Michael's eyebrows climb up his forehead as he watches Hector with amusement dancing in his blue eyes. My father, on the other hand, looks everywhere but at me as the color drains from his face. I'm tense, ready to spring into action and grab him if he falls since he looks like he is about to have a heart attack.

"How interesting. I thought you would have seen an angel by now. As a matter of fact, you've seen an angel all your life." Michael's cryptic words only make Hector worse, because now he looks like he's hyperventilating.

"She doesn't know. She doesn't *need* to know! Stop this!" Gasping, Hector grabs the robes he is wearing, pulling at the collar as if it's constricting his breathing. Michael chuckles at his discomfort, and Hector's face goes bright red. "Don't you dare laugh!" he snaps, spittle flying from his mouth while I gape like a fish at him. "You and Raphael thought this was the best way to keep her safe and make sure she picked the right side, so don't you go pointing fingers! I've done everything you've asked and more!" My gasp of shock makes him turn towards me, and I see guilt and pain written all over his face.

"What are you talking about? What does this have to do with what happened?" My voice becomes smaller as reality hits me like a bitch slap to my face. "Amanda died because of me? You set her up after she lied to protect me, didn't you? You made sure she died so I would live! Oh my God, you killed her!" Hector's grimace shimmers with guilt, and wide-eyed, I take slow, measured steps away from them both. "Who are you people? What the fuck is going on? Someone better start talking now, or I swear by everything holy I'm going to kill you both!" Pulling my guns, I aim one at Hector and one at Michael. My father pales even more, if that is possible, while Michael eyeballs the gun as if he can make it disappear by looking at it. "Talk!" I wave the guns at their faces.

"You were given to Hector to raise and keep safe because you are half angel. This was the safest place for you," Michael tells me, still squinting at the gun. My knees buckle, and I stiffen my legs so I don't drop on the ground from the shock that hits me like a blow to my chest. My hand trembles slightly pissing me off.

"Why didn't you tell me?" I look accusingly at Hector. "Actually, you know what? Never mind! That doesn't matter right now." Turning away from him while still keeping him at gunpoint, I look at the angel. "And what does that mean exactly, huh? Are you my father?"

"What? No!" Michael looks like I've slapped him, and a sharp pain pierces my chest.

"I'm not that horrible, so don't look like I've insulted you, asshole!"

"Your mother was an angel." He cuts off my tirade, and I close my mouth.

"Is she…alive?" I hate that my voice breaks, so I clear my throat. "Is she still alive?"

"No, she is not." Hector is the one that speaks, and I slowly turn towards him, searching his eyes. "Neither your mother nor your father is alive, Helena." Unshed tears glisten in his eyes, but they turn cold when he looks at Michael. "You better tell her everything since you started this!"

"What more can there be?" I look from one to the other. "My mother was an angel, my father human…" My words trail off when Hector winces. "What?" Snapping the word out, I wave the guns again.

"Your father was a demon." Michael's emotionless voice is like a punch to my solar plexus.

"No!" My scream echoes around the library, bouncing off the walls and sounding like multiple people screaming at once. Fear and anger mix together in a cocktail of such intense emotions that I feel like I might burst into pieces where I stand. "You're lying! I'm not an abomination!"

"You're not, Hel!" Hector tries to comfort me, and the

asshole angel snorts at my nickname. I scowl at him. "No matter what anyone says, you are not an abomination, and no one doubts your loyalty."

"Could've fooled me!" Still sneering at Michael, I backstep, my feet fumbling even though I'm moving slower than a snail. "So, what does this mean?" Alarms blare in my head, the gut feeling in my GPS doubling in its intensity, so much I can't ignore it anymore. *There is definitely something evil here, but how is that possible? Or...am I the evil?* The thought almost makes me double over, but I force myself to keep moving away from them. "Am I evil? Is that why you're here?"

"You are not evil…"

"The demon that scratched you took your blood with him to Hell. They know who and what you are now, and they need your blood to keep the gate open. I cannot let that happen." Michael straightens up, and for the first time, fear grips me like hands squeezing my throat.

He is not a demon or a normal human that I can just fight off. Blessed metal, salt and holy water won't do him harm. No matter how strong I am, there is no way I can fight him and win. So how in the hell am I going to protect myself from him? At the moment, he looks exactly like what he is: a warrior archangel. His blue eyes shimmer like liquid silver, and his blinding-white wings with golden tips spread out around him as he takes a step towards me. Hector screams like a banshee and throws himself at Michael, but the angel only pushes him away one-handed, like he's flicking off lint from his shirt.

"You cannot win this fight, Helena. I should've done this the day we found you, but Raphael is sometimes too sentimental for his own good. I cannot allow you to live. We all must sacrifice for the greater good. Now is just your turn." He takes a step towards me with each word, and I step back. Too late, I realize he has maneuvered me around so that my back is now facing the window instead of the door.

"You will excuse me for not agreeing with that statement when I'm the one that has to die because *you* think it's for the greater good? I've done nothing wrong!" My eyes flick to Hector, but he is crumpled on the floor, unconscious. There's nothing I can do to help him at the moment. Hell, I can't even help myself!

"You can try to fight the inevitable, but…"

Michael's words are cut off by a thunderous boom and the shattering of a window. Hunching my shoulders on reflex, I watch in slow motion as tiny pieces of glass, sparkling in rainbow colors as they fly through the air around me, not touching me anywhere like I'm in some sort of a bubble, fly at the Archangel. A roar shakes the walls of the sanctuary when all of them embed themselves in both of his outstretched wings, and I drop my guns to cover my ears. When I pull my hands away, they're covered in blood, but I can't worry about that because the green-eyed monster boy I saw when Amanda died flips through the window like an acrobat and bounces on the tips of his toes next to me. I forgot how handsome he was after he disappeared in the shadows, but like a slap to my cheek, I'm reminded now. He's trying to say something, but I can't hear a word, so I just lift my hands towards him dumbly, showing him the blood. He looks down at my hands and frowns before his head snaps to look at something. My gaze follows his as I search to find what pulled his attention away.

Michael is slowly lifting himself up, looking at both of us with murder written all over his perfect, angelic face. The golden glow around him crackles and sparks fly in all directions, making my skin feel like it's burning even from this distance. Something taps my arm, and I look back at my savior. His green eyes bore into mine as if looking for something, and after a second, he turns towards the shattered window. I twist around as well, looking at what he's doing. The Archangel is about to kill me anyway, so some part of me decides to check out the handsome guy's ass, and of course it makes me jealous of his leather pants. He waves his hand in my line of vision and my eyes snap to his face. With a smirk, he reaches his hand towards me. I remember his warning earlier in the night when he told me he wouldn't show up the third time I need him to guard my back. His eyes flick to something behind me every two seconds, but he's not leaving or hurrying me along. He just stands there, his hand palm up and within arm's reach. I know I might regret it if I take him up on his offer, but at the moment, he is giving me at least one more day to live. If I'm alive, I can try to figure this out. Or, so I hope.

Looking over my shoulder, I see Michael already up on one knee, shimmering blood seeping from his wings, making them look red instead of the beautiful white they are. The hatred on his face tells me he wants to rip me limb from limb, so without overthinking it too much, I reach my hand out and wrap my fingers around warm, calloused ones. The stranger pulls me with him and out the window as yet another roar shakes the walls. The pressure in my head is too much, and before I say a word, my eyes roll to the back of my head.

Chapter Twelve

A groan passes my lips as I bury my face in the pillow that smells so good I think I never want to leave the bed. Wrapping my arms around it, I pull it closer, pushing my nose into it and inhaling deeply. Suddenly, the pillow vibrates, freaking the hell out of me. With a squeak that I might find embarrassing if anyone hears it, I throw myself away from it. I misjudge the force I put behind the push and teeter on the edge of the bed for a second, flailing my arms before gravity pulls me down where I slam against the floor on my ass and hip with an audible thud.

"Ouch!" Groaning again, this time in pain, I flip onto

my back and start rubbing my hip while staring at the ceiling.

My hand freezes when I notice all the constellations and planets that are painted on it. The ceiling is black, and the beautiful colors of the planets and stars make it seem like I'm actually looking into space. This is definitely not my room. It takes me a moment to hear the chuckling coming from the top of the bed, and with dread pooling in the pit of my stomach, painfully and slowly, I lift myself up just enough so that my eyes are peeking over it. They widen in shock when they connect with green ones, and I watch the monster boy fight his laughter while his entire body shakes with the effort.

As if my gazing at him gives him permission, he throws his head back and booming laughter bursts out of him. It shakes the entire bed he is stretched out on, and my face must be a ton of different shades of red when I realize, mortified, that there are no other pillows on it apart from the one under his head. I'd been clinging to him like some addict, and I plop back down on the floor and cover my face with my hands, trying to hide my humiliation.

"This can't be happening!" I mumble through my hands before panic grips me, forcing me to pat my body to ensure I'm still fully clothed. "Thank God I'm not naked," I mumble. Finally, I take a calming breath. The laughter stops like someone turned off the sound.

"Your God had nothing to do with it! I would never

undress you, not until you beg me to do it, cupcake." His deep voice makes my insides vibrate, and I'm angry that he affects me like this.

"Keep dreaming, monster boy. I wouldn't hold my breath if I were you." I'm still on the floor because obviously I'm a coward and can't face him just yet. My heart stutters at the realization of what I don't touch when I'm making sure I'm still dressed. "My guns!" Jerking my body up, I scramble to lift myself up.

"Calm down. I grabbed them as soon as I realized you were hurt and your ears were bleeding. Somehow, I had a feeling they were important to you." His eyes sparkle with amusement when I sag in relief. "Not bad for a monster boy, huh?"

The entire day yesterday crashes in on me like a boulder and wariness takes over. I watch him closely, and he doesn't shy away from my penetrating stare. He only searches my gaze while my eyes stay locked on him, and he doesn't even reply with a smartass comment like he does every time I've laid eyes on him so far.

"Why are you helping me?" Narrowing my eyes, I wait to see if anything, even a flicker of something that will confirm he's the monster I know he is. "What are you hoping to gain?"

"Not everyone has to want something to help a pretty girl like you, cupcake." He frowns at me as if I insulted him somehow." Some of us just like to do the right thing.

Is that so hard to believe? I thought that's what they teach you in that shithole you call home."

"You're a demon!" He opens his mouth to say something, but I talk over him, staring him down. "Don't deny it! I saw your eyes when you were fighting the others!" Pointing a finger in his face, I glare at him. "Don't you dare lecture me about doing the right thing!"

"And how exactly is it forbidden for me do the right thing? Is that something reserved just for certain species, or…" One of his eyebrows goes up, and for a moment I'm rendered speechless while staring at his face. It should be illegal for anyone to be this handsome.

Blinking a few times to get my head out of the gutter, I frown at him. "You're a demon!" I tell him slowly, like he is stupid and that statement explains everything.

"And you're a *human*." He drags the word out, mimicking me while I wince at his assumption, which causes anger to bubble in my chest.

"It's what you abominations never do! The right thing is not what you are born to do. It's just not in you!" Agitated, I pace up and down the front of the bed.

"Oh, really?" It stings my ego that he looks more handsome when he's angry, like right now as he stares intently at me and his eyes turn a darker green than their usual color. "And what exactly, oh pure one, am I born to do? Pray tell me so I never mistake my place again!"

I know that I'm talking out of my ass right now, but I'm angry, hurt, confused, and most of all freaked out by the hold he has on me. So instead of dealing with it like a mature adult, I try my best to hurt him and insult him, but for what? Because he keeps his word and has my back when those I call my own turn their weapons on me to my face? Regardless of all that, I can't stop the crap that keeps coming out of my mouth. Because if I do, I'll be admitting that my entire life has been a lie. That I am as much of an abomination as the ones I've been hunting my whole life. That my best friend died to protect an evil creature that doesn't deserve to live. I'm not sure I can handle it all in this moment.

"You guys are evil. You use, abuse, and kill humans for nothing but your own amusement. We're the opposite of you and we protect humanity. It's how life works, monster boy. Don't shoot the messenger!" Crossing my arms over my chest, I look at him sternly, like he is some disobedient child.

"You're good?" He laughs humorlessly, shaking his head. "I never said demons are good. I said *I* did the right thing. Demons are not all bad, just like not all of you are good. Sorry to burst your bubble. We hunt the rogues as much as you do. The only difference is we don't kill everything that's not part of our order. You know"— Waving his hand at me, his lips stretch into a sinister smile —"like what you do. If it's not part of the order or human, kill it first, ask questions later. Right? Because that doesn't make you as much of a monster as I am, cupcake."

79

"Stop calling me cupcake!" I cry out, turning away from his penetrating stare. His words are like a punch to the gut. "My name is Helena, but you can call me Hel."

"Eric." At the sound of his name, I peer over my shoulder at him.

"Eric." I test the sound of his name on my lips, and his eyes turn hot, like they'll burn me to ashes where I stand. "It suits you." Unable to look away from his eyes, I try to remember how to breathe while butterflies wreak chaos in my stomach. "Why did you help me, Eric?"

"Because from the moment I saw you, there was nothing else I could do but help you, Helena. I tried to stay away, but I ended up following you to your home. There's something about you." Shaking his head as if to clear it, a frown draws his eyebrows together. "I don't know what it is, but it's almost as if I was compelled to protect you. Not that I mind; I just don't like to get involved with the Order. But you're different."

Still looking at his confused and handsome face, a deep sigh passes my lips, making his frown deepen. "Different? You have no idea, monster boy."

Chapter Thirteen

Sitting on a stool, leaning over the kitchen counter, I watch Eric as he cooks breakfast. My mind is in shambles and I have a pounding headache, making my temples throb with their own heartbeat. My best friend's unseeing eyes keep flashing behind my eyelids almost every time I blink and the pain in my chest feels like someone has hit me with a sledgehammer when I remember Hector has something to do with it. Persistently, I keep pinching my thigh in hopes that all of this is a horrible nightmare and I'll finally wake up to Amanda telling me I'm having a nightmare because I'm suppressing my emotions. Everything feels surreal, especially remembering Archangel Michael standing in front of me with his outspread wings. I'm not really sure why I find that specific detail to be so unbelievable. I mean, I hunt demons, for goodness sake. Why on earth do I find angels shocking?

"Stop biting your nails." Eric's deep voice jolts me out of my thoughts, and I realize that I'm biting my nail so hard my finger is about to start bleeding.

He doesn't even turn around when he speaks. It is like he has eyes in the back of his head. He's still flipping eggs and thick pieces of bacon on the gas-burning stove that looks like it belongs to a restaurant, not a home kitchen, the delicious aroma filling the air around me and making my stomach twist in knots. Just like the bedroom, the kitchen is in dark colors. It's a modern setup that's sleek and elegant with marble countertops and glossy black cabinets reflected on the dark silver appliances, which I find surprising for a single guy. My mind stops with a screech. Is he single? And what the hell do I care whether he is or isn't? My eyes flick towards him, and a tingle in my belly makes me clench my teeth when I can't seem to look away. The bastard refuses to put a shirt on, and there he stands, barefoot and clad only in sweatpants. His bare back has no right to look as sexy and tempting as it does. With each movement, I discover new muscles that I didn't know existed on someone's back. He's not bulky like some bodybuilder, but he has enough definition that it's almost like watching a piece of art when he moves. My eyes trace the exposed skin all the way to his narrow waist, his low-slung sweatpants barely hanging on, and my mouth dries up the longer I keep looking at him. His full sleeve of tattoos etched on his right arm just adds to the enigma that he is. The clearing of a throat makes my eyes jerk up, and I groan at his smirk and the amusement in his eyes. Busted!

"What?" I scowl at him as if it's his fault that I can't control my hormones around him.

"How do you like your eggs?" Chuckling, he looks back to what he's doing, and it takes me a second for the words to register in my brain. The muscles on his arm bunch up, drawing my eyes to them as he moves his hair out of his face. I'm wondering if he's doing it on purpose to mess with my head. I don't know him at all, but I'm almost ready to bet my life that he is.

"Sunny side up, please." My voice comes out a little too breathless for my liking, but I cover it up by clearing my throat. "You don't have to cook for me. I'd be happier if you give me information much more than I'd appreciate food at the moment."

"Breakfast is the most important meal of the day. Plus, you could use some food after everything you went through yesterday. First, we eat, and then we talk."

"Okay, Mother!" At my bitchy comment, he only chuckles, shaking his head as he starts piling food on plates.

Setting the plate in front of me, he takes the seat at my side, and starts eating without saying another word. After scrutinizing the food and feeling uncomfortable for a few moments, I follow his lead and dive in. I didn't feel hungry, but after the first bite, it feels like I haven't eaten in a month, and an embarrassing moan passes my lips as I chew on the bacon. Eric doesn't say anything, but pauses for a second, looking at me out of the corner of his eye, then his nostrils flare as if he is scenting the air. My stomach flipflops at that and I swallow my food fast, gulping half the glass of orange juice he places in front of me.

"The bacon is delicious." Breaking the silence, I'm hoping I'll stop feeling like I want to jump out of my skin from his nearness. His lips twitch at my words, but he keeps his face stoic as he pretends that I'm not staring daggers at him.

Not looking away from his plate, he prods the eggs. "That's because it's not bacon. It's human meat." His face is emotionless, not giving anything away. He doesn't blink an eye about what he just said and takes another bite of his food.

"*What?*" My voice echoes around the kitchen as I jump off the stool, turning around in a panic to look for somewhere to empty my stomach.

A burst of booming laughter startles me out of my flustered state, and I freeze, my eyes widening and landing on him. "You should've seen your face!" He pounds his fist on the counter and tears glisten from the corners of his eyes. "Really, Helena. You don't believe a word I say, but you believe that I actually cooked you a human? I'm not sure if I should laugh or cry at that."

"Well, you are a…"

"A monster? Yeah, I know," he cuts me off dryly." Or…no! An abomination. That's right!"

"I was going to say a demon!" With a sigh, I press the heels of my hands to my forehead. "This whole situation is so fucked up," I mumble as I reclaim my seat.

"Not really. You're only now finally looking past the blinders and the brainwashing they give you in the Order. You say demon like it's an insult." Lifting an eyebrow, he glances at me for a second. "It's like me calling you human in hopes of hurting your feelings."

"It's not the same!" Pushing the plate away, I glower at him.

"No? What's the difference?"

"Abominations are evil! They kill, abuse, and eat humans for fuck's sake! A demon is not the same as a human!"

"Humans do worse things to each other. I'm a demon, and I haven't yet sampled a human. So according to you, I should try one, huh?"

"So you say!" At my response, he looks at me for a few long moments before shaking his head.

"No matter what I tell you, you won't believe me." With a deep sigh, he pulls my plate closer to my seat. "Eat!"

"No!" Stubbornly, I cross my arms over my chest.

"Don't you want to see and hear for yourself what the reality really is?"

"What do you mean, *hear* and *see*?" Forgetting all about my anger, I watch him closely.

"I'll show you instead of telling you. That way you won't need to believe my words. You can believe your own eyes."

"Okay, let's go!" Jumping off the stool, I spin, but midway his tongue clicks, stopping me.

"Nope!" Tapping the plate with his fork, his pointed gaze meets mine. "First you eat! Then we go!" Without another word, he focuses on his food again, ignoring me even as I stare at him with my jaw hanging open.

Seeing that I won't win this argument, I grumpily sit back on the stool and shovel food in my mouth. It's amazingly delicious, but I'll be damned if I tell Eric that. For whatever reason, he affects me more than any other attractive man I've seen in my life, and there are plenty of those at the Sanctuary. Something is going on, and I'd better find out what before I do something stupid. Like start touching him the way I really want to right now, when he is sitting so close that I can feel his body heat through my clothing.

Chapter Fourteen

I'm not the least bit surprised when we step out of the skyscraper that Eric lives in and head right up to a sleek black Porsche, a valet next to it holding the door open for us. I don't know Eric at all, but even without seeing his ride, I'd assumed it'd be either something fast or a motorcycle. He definitely doesn't look like someone that drives a sedan or a minivan. Snorting at my own thoughts, I see him turn his head slightly my way with a raised eyebrow, but I ignore him. Watching him parade around half-naked for over an hour, then having to see him moving through his place with his leather pants unbuttoned, his boxers peeking out from under them, and his to-die-for abs taunting me when he pulled a shirt on—

a procedure that looked more like undressing then dressing up—had been enough to mess me up for a lifetime. So, I decided to ignore him, like he didn't even exist, instead thinking of Solomon or Samuel every time my mind pictured his body again. That was enough to snap me out of my lusty thoughts.

The day is beautiful, but the warm breeze rustling my hair and tickling my face like a gentle touch does nothing to calm my anxiety. I have no idea where he's taking me, but I know deep in my gut that it'll only confirm all the shit that happened last night. The kid standing next to the car looks about sixteen or seventeen, and his eyes widen comically when he sees me walking next to monster boy. I can only imagine what he's thinking, looking at the cargo pants, buckled knee-high boots, and the dozen belts looped around my waist and thighs with my two guns attached to them. My taste in clothing has always been more peculiar then anyone else's in the sanctuary, but I've never felt self-conscious about it until now. I've never roamed around the city in the morning or during the day, either, so that might be why. Self-consciously, I smooth my hands over my hair and wipe my palms on my thighs.

"How are you, sir?" the valet kid smiles broadly at Eric while his eyes keep flicking in my direction.

"Good, Jim. How are you? School almost over for the year?" Eric smiles at the kid, and the conversation is so ordinary that I almost stumble over my own feet from the absurdity of it. The guy is a demon for fuck's sake.

"Yeah…umm…just about," Jim stutters, his cheeks turning pink as if he's embarrassed that Eric remembers details about him.

"Thank you for bringing her over." Clapping the kid on the shoulder a couple of times, Eric slides into the car gracefully, and dumbfounded, I follow suit—if a lot less gracefully—closing the door gently in case I damage it or something. It looks brand new, the smell of leather so strong inside that I had a feeling it had just come from the dealership.

Jim is still smiling like he has won the lottery because Eric talks to him when the car purrs to life and we peel away from the side of the road. I watch the kid in the side mirror until I can't see him anymore, then I shift my body towards my companion, my eyebrows almost touching my forehead. He doesn't look at me, but keeps his eyes locked straight ahead, weaving in and out of traffic like a Formula 1 driver.

"What?" After a while of me staring, his baritone breaks the silence, but he still doesn't glance in my direction.

"That was quite…" Lost for a proper word to use, my voice trails off.

"Human?" His full lips twitch again, and the corners of his eyes crinkle as if he is suppressing a smile. "Maybe I should've eaten him. You know, to live up to the reputation and all." Lifting his hand, he scratches his five o'clock shadow as if contemplating it.

"That's not funny!" Huffing at him, I turn away and look out the window at the blurring scenery zooming past us. "None of this makes sense. Demons are grotesque-looking evil creatures who are trying to destroy humanity. They don't talk, much less look and act like you."

"Why, Helena! That almost sounded like a compliment!" Sarcasm is thick in his words, and I glance at him from the corner of my eye.

Since I don't know what to say, I rub my hands over my face, praying my headache will go away. I'm still wearing the same clothes I put on yesterday morning, and I washed my face without having my makeup or anything else with me, making me feel exposed and vulnerable. A wary sigh escapes me and I huff at my own stupidity. My whole life has turned to crap, my best friend is dead, my father has lied to me and might have something to do with her death, an archangel is on my ass trying to kill me, and a demon has saved my life. Rationally, I doubt that not having makeup is my biggest problem at the moment, but I cling to it in hopes everything else will just go away like it didn't happen. If I am honest with myself, I might admit that I wear it like war paint in hopes that it will mask my fragile heart and emotions. It's been working well until now.

"Listen, all jokes aside…no, I suppose it's not funny at all. That being said, the situation is what it is. Nothing can change it. You'll just have to make the best of it." Sobering up, he turns his handsome face my way, and when I look at him, my stomach clenches at the pity in his green eyes.

"Don't pity me, monster boy!" Through clenched teeth, I growl angrily at him. "And watch the damn road! I didn't cheat death last night only to die in a car crash!" Grabbing the leather seat underneath me, I dig my fingers into it, breathing through my nose in hopes to ground myself and stop the panic that is trying to overwhelm me. "I don't need your pity! I'm not some helpless girl you found on the side of the road that requires saving." Staring him down, I'm not surprised that he is still watching me intently while driving like a bat out of hell. "I don't have a sad story to tell you that I have been unloved or mistreated. My life was perfect until a week ago. This whole thing is like a horrible nightmare that I'm waiting to wake up from."

"I don't pity you…"

"Could've fooled me!" Grumbling, I turn away from him. "Where are we going, anyway?" When he doesn't answer, I look at him, and after a few moments of searching my eyes, he looks at the road again.

"We are almost there," is all he says, after which silence drapes heavily in the car.

Flying sideways through three lines of traffic like there are no other cars around us, Eric gets off the highway and drives to downtown Atlanta. Skyscrapers stretch up towards the sky, blotting out the sun, and thousands of people weave in and out of the buildings and businesses alike. We enter an underground parking garage and it takes my eyes a second to adjust to the abrupt change of light, even as I blink rapidly to speed up the process. When I can finally see, my heart skips a beat because he's driving us straight towards a wall. My breath gets stuck in my throat as my eyes shut instinctively and I brace for impact. When nothing happens, I peel one eye open while my heart hammers in my chest so hard I think it can physically be seen through my clothing.

"What in the actual fuck is this?" I breathe, gaping at what looks like a parking lot for an agency or something from a crime show.

Black SUVs are lined up on one side with people standing around them chatting. Turning around, I look over my shoulder and see that the wall is still there, but we somehow drove through it without dying. A million questions are spinning through my head, but I'm in so much shock right now that I'm not sure I'm capable of speaking, so I just gulp down the panic and stare at what's around me. Opposite the SUVs is an entrance with automatic glass double doors that keep opening and closing as if it's the busiest place in town. What the hell is going on? Gawking, it takes me a moment to realize we're parked between a Harley and a bright yellow Ferrari while Eric is sitting, leaning his back against the door with his arms crossed over his chest, watching my reaction.

"Where have you brought me?" Even I can hear the

panic and accusation in my voice, and I wince at showing him how freaked out I am by all this.

"We're still in Atlanta. I brought you with me to work." His green eyes watch my face so intently I squirm in the leather seat.

"What was the wall thing over there? How did you go through it?" Narrowing my eyes, I'm hoping my anger will mask the fear gripping my heart at the moment.

"It's just a glamour. An easy trick we can do with wards." Waving his hand nonchalantly, as if he just said the weather is nice, he opens the door and climbs out. I'm still staring at the spot he occupied, frozen in place. "Come on, let's go."

"Why am I here?" Suspicion is making me act like a coward, but I can't help myself. This is the last thing I need at this point.

"To see that everything is not as black and white as you were made to believe." Leaning down to look at me, bracing both hands on the roof of the car, Eric smiles mischievously as his hair falls down, covering half his face "I won't let anyone eat you, I promise. I can't promise I won't try, though." Winking at me, he straightens up and closes the door before jogging around the front of it with his eyes on me.

Clenching my fists, I sneer at his stupid smiling face through the windshield and gather my wits about me. I came all the way here like some idiot, so I might as well see what's going on. The weight of my guns pressing on my thighs feels like a comforting hug, which helps to slow down my overly fast heartbeat. I've never missed a target in my life, and I can get out of here if I need to, so I should stop freaking out and deal with it. Hopping out of the car, I slam the door a lot harder than necessary, making him wince.

"Let's go, then! Lead the way." Lifting my chin stubbornly, I watch him shake his head and sigh before I follow him inside the building. And yes, I did shamelessly keep my eyes on the round globes of his ass, mesmerized by the black leather pants hugging it, which again makes me envy that material.

Chapter Fifteen

My feet slow down on their own when we enter what looks like a reception area. The floor tiles are scuffed by what appears to be many walking shoes, and the cracks make random patterns on the floor. The walls look freshly painted with a few paintings of pastures and mountains hanging here and there, making it look so ordinary it's almost ridiculous and absurd. There is a door leading further into the building on my right and a semicircle desk in front of me with two fake-potted trees on either side of it. A young, dark-haired woman, with her hair wrapped in a tight bun and a silky red shirt, sits behind it, her gaze locked on the computer screen until she lifts her head and a smile spreads across her lips when she spots Eric. That same smile slips, turning into a frown when she notices me next to him.

"Loren, how are you?" Eric grins as he greets her, and her brown eyes turn to him.

"As good as ever, Eric. How are you?" she purrs. Her eyes flick to me when she says it, suggesting it wasn't simply a polite thing for her to say to him.

"Same old. Is Maddison here yet?" Ignoring her hints, he leans on the desk, casually pulling me closer to him by the belts around my hips. The woman doesn't miss this action, and her eyes narrow at me. It's so surreal that I just stand there, letting monster boy handle me like an object while all I can do is blink.

"Yeah, she just got here a few minutes ago with her entourage. Should I let her know you're here? And who should I say you are with?" One pencil-thin eyebrow raises in question.

Rapping his knuckles on the desk twice, startling me out of my skin, Eric pulls himself up to his six-foot-something height. "Nah, I'll just go right in. Thanks!" Giving Loren's startled face a crooked smile, he puts his hand on my lower back, turning me around and leading me towards the closed door. As he pulls one side open and ushers me to enter in front of him, I peer over my shoulder. Loren is staring daggers at my back, but before I can be sure that her eyes were starting to glow with a yellowish light, the door closes behind me. Surprisingly, my gut GPS stays silent, not alerting me to anything evil. It's the only reason I go obediently where he's leading me.

"Your girlfriend is not happy you're touching me." Stepping sideways, I make him drop his hand to his side. We're in a long, empty hallway with many doors on each side. At the far end are double doors with a nameplate on one side, too far away for me to read.

"What are you talking about?' Frowning, he strides towards the double doors with purpose.

"Loren didn't look happy you were touchy-feely," I drawl as I speed up my steps to keep up with him. I don't know why I'm saying these things, because I couldn't care less what he does, but I can't stop the words pouring out of my mouth. *Maybe I am possessed,* I think gloomily to myself.

Eric chuckles and decides to ignore my snarky comments, for which I'm grateful. At least one of us is using his brain today. We walk in silence for a bit, and as we near the double doors at the end of the hallway, they crack open as if sensing our presence. My heart speeds up at this, and I become very alert to every sound in the hall, or lack thereof. I don't notice until this very moment that it's unusually quiet here, like in a soundless chamber. My feet slow down and then stop a few steps away from the partly-opened door.

"Good morning!" Eric strides right through it, pushing it all the way open with his shoulder, but I stay where I am.

"Any news?" A woman's musical voice sounds from inside, making my body relax from the position I stand in.

"We'll see." Finally, there's a sound like someone is pulling up a chair, and a deep sigh follows it. "Come inside, cupcake. No one is going to eat you here." Anger pokes its ugly head up at his words. He'll never let me live that down, it seems.

Squaring my shoulders, I strut inside the office, not closing the door. "And who do we have here?" The musical voice belongs to the most beautiful woman I've ever seen in my life. Thick waves of bright red hair fall around her shoulders and down her back. Smooth, almost airbrushed, skin covers her high cheekbones, a button nose, and pouty reddish lips that look naturally colored. Just seeing her perfect face and blue eyes, so bright they look fake, tells me there is no way in hell she's human. She's sitting behind a large, dark mahogany desk that should belong to a museum, not an office, as I assume this is. No one can be that perfect. Of their own accord, my eyes flick to Eric's smiling, stupidly handsome face. Yup! Not human!

"Maddison, meet Helena." There is laughter in Eric's voice, and I have no doubt it's because I'm gaping like an idiot at the beauty in front of me.

A movement from behind her gets my attention, and at that same second whatever spell she had me under shatters. Pulling my guns with both hands, I point them in the faces of the two men standing behind her. I don't know their names, but I will never forget those faces. Eric jumps from the seat he has taken, but the woman just watches me intently, not batting an eyelash over the guns pointed in her direction.

"What the fuck is going on here?" I snap at Eric, not taking my eyes off the men in front of me. "You two are dead!"

"Is that what they told you, Hel?" The blond hunter I've seen around sanctuary my whole life quirks a smile. "They said we're dead?" He looks at the dark haired one standing next to him. They were team members, and we were told they died on a mission six months ago. They look very much alive to me.

"You brought a hunter here, Eric?" Maddison lifts an eyebrow in question, but she doesn't look one bit worried if that's the case.

"She's not a hunter anymore." Eric's words make the two presumably dead hunters gawk at him like he just sprouted horns. My stomach tightens in knots. "Michael tried to kill her last night inside their sanctuary."

"Interesting!" Her eyes narrow at me like she's trying to read my mind. "Why would Michael bloody his hands when he has others doing his dirty work for him?" Her words sound like she's thinking out loud, not asking a question.

"That's what's been bothering me as well," Eric answers anyway. "I figured that if anyone can convince her that not everything is like what they tell them in that damn Order, it'd be you. I didn't even think of Marco and John."

"It's a trap!" The blond hunter snaps and, pulling a small crossbow out, he points it at my chest. "She's everyone's favorite in the Order. There is no way Miss Goody Two Shoes isn't a hunter. She's their perfect pupil. Their *creation*."

My guns are still pointed at their faces, and we have an awkward standoff in this not-so-large office, but Eric and Maddison look bored with the whole display. I can't deny that seeing the two men I assumed were dead gives my mind whiplash, and this entire thing is made worse by my gut feeling staying quiet. There is not even a tingle or a hint that there is evil around me. That means they are not possessed or turned evil. They just look pissed and, if I'm not mistaken, scared of me.

"Why would you bring her here?" the dark haired one asks Eric, glaring at him.

"I'm not joking. Michael did try to kill her. She would've been dead if I hadn't pulled her out of there." Eric stares straight at Maddison when he speaks, totally ignoring the two men and their ramblings.

"Why would he do that, Helena?" Her voice pulls my attention to her, taking my eyes off the two hunters across from me.

They both jump towards me as soon as I look away like they've been waiting for the distraction. I can't say I blame the hunters because I would've done the same. You never take your eyes off your target. The sound of the arrow being discharged from the crossbow sings in the air and I twist my body, pirouetting, letting it pass an inch from my chest. It rips my jacket off, but at least it's not embedded in me. I haven't yet stopped the movement of my body when a blur of action happens and both hunters are unconscious in a heap on the floor with Eric standing over them with murder in his eyes.

"It gets even more interesting," Maddison muses, not blinking an eye at the shit going on around her. "Why would the Archangel want to kill you?"

This time it's not just words coming out of her mouth, it's a demand for an answer, and I'm tired of all the crap that keeps happening around me. Re-holstering my guns with a heavy sigh, I drag my feet up to the closest chair and plop down into it, scrubbing my hands over my face.

"Because I'm not human." At my words, Eric's head snaps in my direction, forgetting all about the two men at his feet. "I'm half angel"—Maddison frowns at that — "and half demon." My eyes lock on Eric's and the shock there is unmistakable.

"My, oh my! Life just got very, very interesting, cousin!" A huge smile spreads over Maddison's face and her eyes turn pure white, glowing with excitement.

Chapter Sixteen

The office is so quiet you can hear a pin drop. My eyes flick from Eric's face to Maddison's white, glowing eyes, my heart beating erratically in my chest while my head continues to pound, gaining intensity until it's bordering on a migraine. I've never had headaches in my life, apart from a few that were a result of a little concussion I'd gotten while training. It must be the stress of the week piling up that's making me want to hit my head against the wall until the pain is more physical, or maybe just until I knock myself unconscious. Looking away from them both, I fiddle with the belts around my hips, avoiding the questions that hang unspoken in the air between us.

"Well, they said…" Clearing my throat uncomfortably and frowning at the buckles like they hold all the secrets in the universe, my quiet voice breaks the silence. "I'm not sure it's the truth. I mean…" Looking up and flicking my eyes from one to the other, I shrug a shoulder. "It seems I've been lied to my entire life. Who's to say they started telling the truth now?"

"That's not possible!" Eric's voice slices like a whip, making me flinch from the barely-contained anger in his words.

"What do I have to gain by lying to you, monster boy?" Snapping at him through clenched teeth, I try my best not to pull a gun out and put a bullet between his beautiful green eyes. Maddison chuckles like this whole thing, my life going to shit, is amusing her to no end. I send a withering stare at her next, and her smile only grows, making me wonder if her perfect cheeks are hurting from how wide her mouth is stretched.

"You don't get it, cupcake! It's impossible, because all hybrids like that, half angel, half demon, are dead. The Archangels never let them live more than a few days before they are discovered and killed." Crossing his arms over his impressive chest that's straining the fabric of his t-shirt to its limits, he looks down his nose at me.

"Stop fucking calling me cupcake!" Rage surges in my chest and my body lifts from the chair as if I'm readying myself to attack him, which isn't far from how I feel. "I said that's what Michael told me before he tried to attack.

I want nothing to do with the demons, nor do I have anything in common with the abominations." Deflating with a deep sigh, I scrub my hands over my face again, as if that will make this whole nightmare go away. "I pray I have nothing in common with them." My whispered words behind my hands weren't as quiet as I thought. A growl rumbles from Eric's chest, making my head snap up to look at him.

He's still standing behind Maddison's desk on top of the two unconscious hunters, and my eyes flick to her face. The white is gone, her eyes going back to their unnaturally blue color, and her perfect face is set in a frown that doesn't take away from how beautiful she is. Tilting her head to the side, she studies my face for long moments before her eyes travel down, then up my body, studying me as if she's taking my measure but finds me lacking. The thought hits me hard that I don't know anything about these people, and here I am telling them my secrets, putting my life in more danger just by being around them. The familiar feeling of anger washes away my fears and self-pity as I lift myself off the chair and place my hands on my hips.

"Now how about you two tell me who the hell you are, huh? I know you're a demon!" Pointing an accusing finger in Eric's face, his lips twitch in humor at my words, and my fingers jerk with the need to slap it off his handsome face. "But who are you, Maddison? Or more importantly, *what* are you? Monster boy here said I would see for myself that I've been lied to. The only thing I've found out so far is that these two traitors are still alive. Apparently switching sides is a thing now. Nothing else!" Agitated, I wave my hand in the direction of Eric's feet, and as if on command, a pained groan comes from the tangled hunters on the floor as they start moving sluggishly.

"You didn't tell her anything?" Maddison looks over her shoulder at Eric, who only shakes his head slowly before lifting his hand to his face and scooping the hair that's fallen over it, pushing it away from his eyes. My gaze follows the movement, almost like it's connected to him by an invisible thread. It pisses me off to no end, but I can't seem to stop myself.

"She thinks demons don't talk. That they just all look grotesque and eat humans." They glance at each other, and their expression is one I can't decipher. When their eyes turn to me with intent, dread pools in my stomach. "How do you explain something to someone who refuses to look past her prejudices and beliefs?" Shaking his head sadly, his shoulders drop a fraction as if he feels defeated, and that confuses the hell out of me. "She's not ready to see the truth, no matter what I tell her. I thought you'd have better luck. A word of caution, though, she's more stubborn than a mule." Winking at me, he walks past me and around the desk, dropping into the chair he occupied when he first stepped inside the office.

"What made you think that demons don't talk?"

Maddison's musical voice makes my eyes snap in her direction and away from Eric, for which I'm thankful because the jerk knows the effect he has on me, and that twitching smile seems permanently attached to his face. I study her face for a moment, but I find only curiosity there, not malice.

Shrugging a shoulder and following Eric's lead, I plop down on my chair. "I've been an active hunter for three years now. I hunt every night to make sure this world is safe from the abominations." Looking intently at her, I expect her to scoff or make a comment, but she only nods slightly as if encouraging me to keep talking. "That's all I've come across, all I've seen and sent back to Hell," I finish after she doesn't interrupt me.

Instead of replying right away, she stares at me for so long that I have to fight the urge to start fidgeting in the chair. "You're sure that's all you've seen?" Her blue eyes penetrate me so hard it's almost as if she can see straight into my soul, and I look away from her only to get locked into Eric's green, intent stare. An unwanted image of the huge black demon with large twisted horns dragging Amanda away comes to my mind as if screaming *liar,* and I flinch internally.

"That was all…" Looking away from Eric's knowing stare, I turn to Maddison. "Until yesterday. First, a new type of demon took my best friend away after he killed her." My eyes flick to Eric. "Then monster boy here came to my rescue for whatever reason"—He gives me a sad smile, making my insides twist, so I look away from him — "twice. He came to my rescue twice."

Nothing seemed to faze the beautiful woman sitting behind the large desk until now. At my words, her perfectly shaped eyebrows hit her hairline and her blue eyes widen comically as her head snaps in Eric's direction, then her mouth opens slightly as if she is in shock. Frowning, I turn to look at Eric as well, only to realize he is not paying attention to Maddison at all. His focus is centered so intensely on me, it causes a shiver to pass up and down my spine, making me hyperaware of his nearness. Goosebumps cover me from head to toe at his complete attention. Caught like a deer in headlights, I can't seem to pull my gaze away from him no matter how hard I try, even while alarms blare inside my head that nothing good can come from having his full attention. After what feels like an eternity, he releases me from whatever spell he has me under and turns to Maddison, shrugging his shoulder nonchalantly, not concerned at all that the woman seems like she is frozen from the shock of my revelation.

"We're getting off track here." Another unspoken conversation passes between them, making me push away my internal debates to narrow my eyes at them. Maddison snaps out of her shock, too, and now she has her full attention on me with a whole new interest that I'm not sure I like. "I believe she asked who, or what, you are," he tells her.

"Yes, I believe she did." Maddison starts talking, but two heads pop up from behind her, startling me so much I'm out of the chair with my guns pointed at the hunters before I am aware I've moved.

"She is Lilith's daughter." The blond hunter groans as he lifts himself up and turns to help his friend like he didn't just drop the biggest bomb of the century.

Icy dread grips my chest, and fear squeezes my heart at his words. Without thinking, I turn both my guns from the hunters and point them at the biggest threat in the room. Maddison.

Chapter Seventeen

I'm not sure why the disappointment I see in her eyes bothers me so much, but I manage to push it down when the handsome jerk to my left chuckles at my reaction. "She doesn't eat humans either," Eric tells me, waving a hand towards Maddison. I'm not sure what kind of a face I make at his words, but he throws back his head, roaring with laughter.

Without thinking, my hand moves, and before I register my reaction, the loud bang of the gunshot echoes in the closed space, making my ears ring. Eric jerks back with the chair he is sitting on while a sizzling noise comes from his right thigh and smoke curls up in front of him.

His handsome face twists in pain and, grinding his teeth, he digs with his claw-tipped fingers, pulling the bullet out before dropping it on the floor with a clink. My eyes follow it as it rolls away, finally stopping Everyone else is frozen in various states of shock, while I watch completely dumbfounded as the blood stops flowing down his leg, his wound closing up, revealing smeared but perfectly smooth skin under the hole in the leather.

"These were my favorite pants." Grimacing and poking the hole with his now-human fingers, he sighs and looks at Maddison, ignoring me like I didn't just shoot him. "See what I mean? She's not ready."

Gaping in disbelief, Maddison eyes never leave me, and judging by the horrified expression on the two hunters' bruised faces, they can't believe what I did. That makes two of us. Looking at the two of them brings back the migraine that has been pushed to the back of my mind by more pressing matters, like Lilith's daughter sitting in front of me and the handsome demon that's messing my mind up with his nearness. Nausea threatens to make the breakfast I ate earlier come right up, so I breathe through my nose in hopes I don't hurl all over his black shitkickers, messing them up along with his pants. The pain comes back with a vengeance, and it almost doubles me over. Everything around me fades into background noise as the swooshing sound of my blood pumping intensifies in my ears, blurring my vision for a second.

Swaying on my feet, I hear it like a distant echo when my guns drop from my numb hands and clatter on the floor before strong arms wrap around me, pulling me tight to a firm chest, and that beautiful scent from this morning envelops me, calming my erratic heartbeat.

Gradually the sound returns as the pain resides, enough for me to be able to hear that everyone in the room is talking at the same time. I can't understand a word they are saying or shouting, but hearing anything must be a good sign. When I look up and my eyes lock on Eric's, my heart flutters for an entirely different reason, and warmth pools in my lower belly when I register how close our faces are from one another. I can feel his warm breath on my face and my lips tingle from his nearness, my fingers tightening on his arms where I've gripped him like he is my lifeline. Worry etches into his features as his eyes search for something I can't put my finger on, but then they zero in on my lips. Subconsciously, I wet them because they feel like I've been stranded in the Sahara for a month without a drop of water, and my tongue sticks to the roof of my mouth when hunger burns in his green gaze. I watch him swallow hard before his eyes slowly meet mine again.

"Are you okay?" His voice is rough and husky, and the hunger is unmistakable. All he has to do is lean in just a little more and our lips will touch. The heat of his body pressed to mine feels like it's seeping through my skin and penetrating my entire being. The strength of how much I want him to close the distance freaks me out so much I jerk away from him so hard he almost releases me, and I know I will drop to the floor if he does because my legs can't hold my weight at the moment.

"I'm fine!" I say, snapping at him like it's his fault I can't seem to resist his pull on me. Gazing at his Adam's apple, I somehow avoid the knowing look I'm sure he has on his stupidly handsome face. When I sneak a glance through my lashes, I don't find the grin I expect. No, his features are softened and my gut clenches at that.

The door opens with a bang, startling me, and I turn my head just in time to see two very tall, muscular men enter the place carrying a sofa like it's a folder full of lightweight papers in their hands, and not a heavy piece of furniture. Dropping it unceremoniously with a thud in the corner of the office next to rows of wooden-framed shelves, they nod towards Maddison and leave without saying a word. Just as the doors are about to close, uneasiness swirls in me when Loren waltzes in, glaring daggers at me. Her silky red blouse is molded to her breasts, and it looks like she unbuttoned a few buttons from the top. The tight pencil skirt is like a second skin hugging her thin frame as her high heels click ominously on the floor as she moves towards me with narrowed eyes, her hips swaying from side to side.

"What's wrong with her?" Loren's voice suggests she is hoping they'll tell her I'm two seconds away from dying, and anger churns in my stomach. I don't know this woman, and whatever her problem is, she can shove it up her tiny little ass. I take a breath to tell her just that when an ominous growl cuts me off, raising the hairs on the back of my neck.

"Loren, get the fuck out!" Eric shouts, snapping my eyes to him. I'm still holding onto him so hard my fingers are digging holes through his shirt when I realize the growl came from him. He's not looking at me anymore, but he is cradling me to his chest protectively as he stares icily at Loren, his eyes glowing the color of amber, like two flames.

"Loren, leave!" Maddison's voice is calm, but when I peer at her over my shoulder, she is not looking at the other woman. No, her eyes are on Eric, a calculating look written all over her pretty face.

Loren stiffens but says nothing as she turns around, lifting her nose so high in the air that I'm not sure how she doesn't trip on those high heels as she struts out of the office like she's walking a runaway.

"No one is going to hurt her, Eric." Maddison's voice is soothing, and unintentionally, even my grip on him loosens. "You have my word. No one will hurt her if I can help it."

"What the hell is going on?" Freaking out because of this whole situation and by my reaction to the demon still holding me in his arms like he will tear anyone apart just for looking at me wrong, I start wiggling so he'll let me go. His arms tighten around me, and his amber eyes land on my face.

"Helena, don't push him away!" Maddison cries out to me, and I swallow my panic at the warning in her voice. "He just needs a moment to collect himself. Don't you, cousin?"

A million thoughts and questions swirl in my mind as I watch Eric struggle with whatever demon he is fighting in his head. A snort escapes me at that particular thought, and those amber flames narrow at me as if he can read my mind. My fear creates all sorts of scenarios in my head, like where he turns into one of the disgusting abominations and starts eating me right here where I stand, and my hands start moving up and down his arms in a soothing motion before I even register what I'm doing. Gradually the glow dims, and I watch, fascinated as his eyes return to their deep green color. I stare at him like some lovesick fool, and we keep staring at each other until a throat clears uncomfortably, breaking the connection.

"How did you know that your touch would calm him?" Maddison looks at me curiously, and I glower at her.

"I want to take her with me tonight." Eric cuts off whatever is going to come out of my mouth as he pulls back from me, hovering close as if expecting me to drop to the floor when he steps away. He's not far from the truth, so I lock my knees to remain standing even though I miss his touch the second he moves away.

"Take me where?" I narrow my eyes suspiciously at him.

"You think that's smart? She can barely stand right now." Maddison is still looking at him as if she expects him to lose his shit at any moment while both of them ignore me like I'm not here.

"She needs to see for herself if she's to stop fighting us at every turn. If what she told us is true, I can't keep her safe if she thinks I'm trying to trick her with everything I say or do." Clenching his fists at his sides as if holding himself back from reaching for me, he turns to Maddison and swallows hard. "If what she says is true…" His voice trails off and Maddison takes a deep breath as if overwhelmed by whatever is left unspoken.

"What just happened…" she begins, looking at him intently, leaning her forearms on the desk, moving her body for the first time since we came into her office. She was sitting unnaturally still for the most part, now that I think about it. "You know what that means…"

"Impossible!" Eric shouts, cutting her off, but his eyes turn in my direction, and my breath catches in my throat at all the emotions swirling in their green depths. "It's not possible." Clearing his throat, he pulls me by my arm and guides me to the sofa, pushing me down until I'm lying flat on it. Dumbfounded, I follow his guidance like some obedient puppy. "I'll figure out what's different about her.

I just need time." He looks at Maddison with determination in his eyes. Before I can ask anything, he glances at me and says one word. "Sleep!"

My eyes close on their own while my brain screams in alarm. It can't be good if he can control me with a single word.

Chapter Eighteen

Voices drift in and out of my consciousness while I'm struggling to wake up for what feels like an eternity. At one point, it sounds like whoever is talking is about to start throwing punches. The voices are angry and loud enough that I almost manage to wake up, but as if they can sense my awareness, they stop, then I drift off to sleep again.

In my dreams, I am chased by the Archangel through the streets of Atlanta, and there is no one around. No cars, humans, or any movement. I keep running as fast as my feet will carry me while glancing over my shoulder to see how close the golden glow of Michael is to me. Everything in downtown is dark apart from a few streetlights scattered here and there, so most of the light comes from the billboards hanging all over the place. I am grateful for the visibility it affords me until I accidently look at one of the billboards. Eric's handsome face looks down on me and his eyes follow my path as if he is keeping an eye on me.

Not stopping my running for fear that Michael will close the distance, I only flick my eyes up every time a new billboard pops up, and Eric's green eyes always keep track of me. For some reason that I refuse to acknowledge, it makes me feel safer. Knowing he is there and will come to my rescue if I need it is more comforting than I expect. Even in my dream, I am aware how ridiculous that feeling is. The guy is a demon, and no matter how hot he is or how my traitorous body reacts to his nearness, I need to remember that. Hector always told me that the devil comes like everything you've ever wanted. Flicking my eyes to the new billboard coming into view, I must admit that those words of wisdom aren't far from the truth. Not far at all! He does look and act like everything I've ever wanted. Hot as Hell—pun intended —he's dark, mysterious, and always there when you need him.

All of a sudden, the glow surrounding Michael closes in around me and I stop running, turning in circles to see which side he is coming from. It gets brighter around me by the second and my eyes flick to Eric's handsome face looming over me and the street. A frown pulls his eyebrows over his eyes as he scans the area around me as well. Pulling my guns out, even when I know they won't kill the Archangel—not that I want to kill him, that's just wrong on so many levels—I grip them tightly because they make me feel more confident, kind of like a safety net. Plus they'd slow him down if it came to that.

"Helena!" Eric's voice booms like all the billboards are calling me at the same time, making me plaster my body to the building in the alley where I'm trying to hide until I spot Michael.

"You can't hide from me, Helena. Not for long!" Michael's voice floats to my ears and shivers rack my frame. He's not yelling or screaming, no. His words are spoken like a promise, not a threat, and fear numbs my brain for a second.

"Helena, open your eyes!" Eric's voice booms again, making me jump a little and snapping me out of the paralyzing fear that has managed to creep up in my head.

"You can't hide her for long, Eric!" Hearing the Archangel addressing Eric makes my eyes widen in shock, until I remember this is my dream and all the stress is making me create these shitty scenarios in my head.

"Helena, wake up!" Eric snaps at me more forcefully, ignoring Michael's words.

"You should just bring her back. If you do, I will forget your insolent behavior from yesterday. She needs to be back in sanctuary. Her father is sick with worry." Michael keeps talking and I almost peel myself off the stone building where I'm pressing my back when he mentions Hector.

"Helena, wake up, NOW!" Eric's forceful yell makes my whole body jerk up and my head connects with something hard, making pain shoot through it.

Someone grunts like they're in pain, but stars flash behind my eyelids and it takes me a moment to open them. When I do, Eric looms over me, rubbing his forehead that's darkening on one side. His eyes search mine even when I'm still a little confused about where I am and whether I'm still dreaming or not. Craning my neck, I look around and reality comes back as a slap in the face when I realize I'm on the sofa in Maddison's office.

"You asshole! You forced me to sleep!" Pushing myself up and making Eric move away so I don't headbutt him again, I narrow my eyes at him. "So much for doing the right thing, huh, monster boy?"

Arching one eyebrow, he looks back at me defiantly, as if daring me to say something more. I want to so bad, but I hold my tongue when I realize there is more worry than defiance in his green orbs. Deflating like a balloon, I allow myself to sink back into the sofa cushions. I've spent most of my life keeping very tight control over my emotions. His nearness is making me lose that hard-earned control in just twenty-four hours.

"Did Michael see you?" Eric's question makes me frown in confusion before my eyebrows hit my hairline.

"How do you know what I was dreaming about?"

Suspicion grows in my stomach. I know nothing of him, and I've been asleep and vulnerable more than I've been awake in his presence. Maybe I have a death wish.

"That wasn't a dream. He entered your subconscious in hopes of finding where you are in reality." He speaks so calm I almost think it's common practice to enter someone else's mind, which makes me just blink at him like I'm a simpleton or something. "Are you okay? Did he see you?" Taking a step closer, his arm moves as if he is reaching for me, but he drops it to his side with a frown when my eyes narrow.

"What else can you do?" Keeping a calm façade, I lift myself off the sofa so I don't have to look up at him.

"Did he see you?" he repeats himself.

"No, he didn't!" Snapping at him, I have to take a calming breath so I can speak again. "What else?"

"What do you mean?" Frowning, he crosses his arms over his chest and widens his stance. I know that tactic, I've used it myself on others when I've felt they are onto my antics.

"You can control me with a word, like compelling me to sleep. You can also enter my mind through visions, as you mentioned. And you were there the time my best friend died as well as when Michael tried to attack me." Looking at him somberly, I mimic his posture. "What else can you do?"

"There is no reason for you to know what else I can do. Not because I feel the need to hide it, but because you need time, Hel. I'm giving you that." Him calling me by my nickname softens something inside me for a moment, and I almost relax under his penetrating eyes.

"Why were you there the night Amanda was killed?" Glaring at him, I snap my words sharply and clench my fists so I don't grab my guns, until I notice they're not in their holsters. "Where are my guns?" At my question, he just points to one of the chairs where my girls are waiting to be picked up. "I won't get distracted, so start talking. Why were you there?" Grabbing the guns, I slide them into their holsters on the outside of my thighs, which instantly makes me feel better.

"I was on a hunt, too." Eric hasn't moved and his eyes track everything, including how many times I blink, I have no doubt. He is too perceptive.

"Hunting the abominations?"

"No."

"Hunting humans?" For some reason, the insides of my stomach twist at the idea of Eric hurting humans.

"No."

Lead pools in my stomach as I search his eyes and silently pray the answer to my next question will be the same. "Hunting Amanda?"

"No."

A huff of air escapes my lungs at his word, and my shoulders slump, releasing the tension coiling inside of me. My lips lift at the corners, but they freeze when I look at his eyes. All emotion vanishes and it looks like he sees me for the first time. Cold sweat beads on my forehead and a shiver passes up my spine.

"I was hunting you," he says it in such a relaxed and emotionless tone that all I can do is mutely stare back at him.

Chapter Nineteen

"You do realize I need more than just 'I was hunting you,' right? Turning away, I move up to the large desk and lean my butt against it. "Since I'm still alive, and you even came to my rescue last night, I'm assuming something changed."

Eric keeps watching me, not giving any hints about what he thinks or feels. I realize that he intentionally allowed me to read his expressions earlier. His admission that he was trying to kill me makes me truly relax for the first time in his presence. His confession eliminates my doubts about being evil. If I'm evil, why would a demon want me dead?

"What I really want to know is who sent you to kill

me," I prod. "And obviously, why you changed your mind."

After looking at me for a few long moments, Eric drops his arms to his sides and turns towards the door. "Let's go, or we will be late." Opening the door, he waits for me to exit first. Pushing off the desk, I slowly move towards him. "We can continue this conversation in the car."

Since acting like an immature brat will only delay the inevitable, I follow him out into the hallway. I don't care where we have the conversation as long as I discover who, apart from the Archangel, is after me. A fleeting memory of Michael addressing Eric by name floats through my mind, but we reach the lobby area and I keep my questions to myself. Loren is staring daggers at us from behind the desk, but Eric doesn't spare her a glance. Striding towards the automatic glass doors, he looks lost in his own thoughts.

I tense when his warm palm settles at the small of my back while he guides me to exit the building in front of him. Watching him from the corner of my eye, I bite my tongue so I don't say anything. Maybe he wasn't as lost in his thoughts as I assumed.

"What's Loren's problem with me?" I blurt out as we near his Porsche.

"What?" Slowing his strides, he looks over, confusion clear on his handsome face.

"Unless she's your girlfriend and doesn't like the idea

of you spending time with another woman, I don't know what her problem is."

My breath hitches as he moves, so fast it's nothing but a blur, pinning me between the side of his car and his body. Goosebumps cover me, and butterflies wreak chaos in my stomach when he cages me with his arms. I'm terrified to move, because if I even allow a muscle twitch, I'm not sure I'll be able to stop touching him. Lowering his head, he brushes my hair away from my face with his nose before sniffing my neck like some hunting dog.

"Maybe it's because you smell delicious." His voice is husky, much deeper than before. I tremble.

"Huh?" Dazed by his nearness, with my heart beating so fast he must feel it on his chest, I try to concentrate on what he is saying.

"Maybe that's her problem," Eric says as he pulls back so I can see his face without my eyes crossing. The demon is too good-looking for my sanity, but I don't push him away.

"Because she is not your girlfriend?" Feeling his hardness pressing on my belly makes my voice breathless, but I'm too gone at the moment to care.

His lips twitch, and hunger stares back at me. Gliding his hand on the car, close enough that he barely touches my body, he grabs my hip and his thumb makes little circles right on my hipbone, driving me insane. "No, she's not."

"Good." I don't look away from him as I wet my suddenly dry lips.

"Look at the little rabbit. It has teeth." His nostrils flare and he presses closer, almost crushing my back on the car.

His smartass comment gives me a little control over my hormones. My eyes narrow.

"What's that supposed to mean?"

"I expected you to push me away, scream bloody murder, or something worse." His lips twitch again, but his eyes are still glued to my lips.

"I'm a hunter for the order, monster boy. I'm not a nun."

His green eyes jerk to mine and amber flakes glow like tiny pinprick stars in them.

My comment dumps a bucket of cold water on my libido. "Or I should say I *was* a hunter. I don't know what I am right now."

Reluctantly, he pulls away, then dips and kisses the corner of my mouth. My brain short-circuits at the touch of his lips. I don't have time to register what happens before Eric guides me to the passenger door, opens it, and pushes me inside. He walks around the car, and I don't look away when he slides in next to me and starts the engine.

"As much as I would like to say that your distraction technique worked"—Clearing my throat, I try to sound less breathless— "I still need to know who sent you to hunt me down."

"I need you to understand that I'll do anything to keep the Order off our back. Well, I would've done anything to keep them off our back. You changed that, and I'm wondering if I doomed us all." Eric glances over before looking straight and pulling out of the parking space.

"What are you saying? And since you were in my head when you forced me to sleep, I'm sure you know that I'm wondering why an Archangel knows you by name."

"You'll know the answer to that question soon enough." He exits the parking garage and the night envelops us. We've been in Maddison's office a lot longer than I thought. I fully expect the first billboard that comes in view to display Eric's face. Instead, some accident injury attorney's face with a huge fake smile stares back.

"Why didn't you kill me?" Changing tactics and watching him from the corner of my eye, I'm hoping he will finally answer something.

"The moment I saw you a week ago standing between a horde of rogue demons and your team, with the headlights of your car behind you like some avenging goddess, I knew I couldn't do it. There is something about you that made me rethink things, even when it means more trouble for us. Maddison was not happy at the time." Shifting in his seat, he steals glances but doesn't look at me. "I decided to get closer to see what's so special about you. Why would the Order agree to let us deal with our own just to get rid of a human hunter? I didn't see it until you were running towards your friend. I could've used your distraction and pain to finish the job, but again I couldn't kill you. Something about you makes me want to protect you, not harm you. The Order wanting you dead and promising to let us deal with our own was enough of a red flag that you are not like the rest of them. I still don't know what makes you different."

"The Order wanted me dead a week ago?" My head spins. If it's true, they wanted me dead the same day the abomination spoke to me and raked my arm. *How would they know?* Were the two events connected, or did they have other reasons for wanting me gone?

Eric says nothing, clutching the steering wheel in a white-knuckled grip and making the metal groan.

"Who was it?" I brace myself for the punch.

"Hector."

My heart shrivels.

Chapter Twenty

After hearing my father, the man who raised me on his own, who wouldn't let a hair on my head fall out of place in fear of it hurting me, wants me dead, thoughts should be screaming through my mind. I want to feel anger, rage, pain, sorrow. Anything at all will do. But I feel nothing. Empty. Of Everything.

I stare out the window, not seeing any of the scenery we pass. Does it even matter? I have spent my entire life doing what is right. I did it to prove that the faith others have placed in me is warranted. Those same people stabbed me in the back, and now I feel empty. Numb.

I'm grateful that Eric doesn't say anything or try to make me feel better. All I'm capable of at this moment is breathing, I can't even feel my heart beating. It's almost like the organ deserts me the moment life shoves me to my knees, only to keep kicking me while I'm still down. A dull ache starts behind my eyes and my ears buzz.

"Stop biting your nails." My head slowly turns towards Eric as he gently pushes my hand down to my lap. "I need you to be alert now, okay? I know the last twenty-four hours have been hard, but at the moment, I need you to be a hunter."

"What do you mean?" Frowning slightly, I try to force my brain to function.

"Things don't look peachy here." He lifts his chin, pointing towards the windshield. I turn to see what's in front of us.

I snap out of the surreal state. We are parked in front of a bar, a dive, actually. The run-down building stands all alone in the middle of nowhere. There are a few cars scattered around the dirt-encrusted parking space. Two poles act like street lights. I say act because the cables hanging from the dangling lights lead to the inside of the bar.

The bar itself appears deserted. No light comes out of it apart from the cracked green-glowing "Hell's Tavern" sign above the door. The door looks ajar, but I can't be sure as shadows obscure one part of the building. The large glass windows seem to have been painted black, I'm assuming to protect the privacy of the patrons. The tin roof is rusted at places, and something oily drips from it.

I focus on what makes Eric wary. Two massive demons with twisted ram horns stand on either side of the two steps leading to the bar's wooden porch. Dressed only in black pants, they stand with their feet shoulder-width apart. Arms as thick as my thighs cross over their large, bare chests, as if they've been waiting for us. Stealing a glance at Eric, I rephrase that thought. Like they've been waiting for *him*, not *us*.

"You're good to go?" He doesn't look at me as we both keep our eyes on the abominations. "I'll do the talking; you just stay close. If anything happens, get to the car. I'll follow right behind you."

"Friends of yours?" The judgment is thick in my voice, but at least he manages to keep me present and alert.

"I wouldn't go that far," Eric mumbles as he grabs the handle and swings the door open, not waiting to see if I'll agree with his request.

By the time I open the door, Eric is almost where the two abominations are standing. I slam the door a lot harder than I intend, disturbing the eerie silence of the parking lot. Wincing internally, I jog to catch up as Eric looks at me over his shoulder. I expect a leer but all I see is concern as he scans me from head to toe, as if making sure I'm okay. A ping in my chest feels like another part of my heart has been shredded.

"I see you brought entertainment, Shadow." The deep voice sounds like rocks grinding together as the abomination on the right chuckles, leering at me. My fingers twitch with the need to grab the girls and put a bullet between his red eyes. *Why is he calling him Shadow?*

"She's none of your concern, Abaddon. What have you learned?" Eric stops in front of them, mimics their posture, and doesn't look at me. My internal GPS goes haywire and makes the hairs on my arms and legs stand straight. I force my legs to keep moving, doing my best to maintain a calm expression on my face.

"Michael has been on a rampage since last night." Abaddon narrows his eyes to slits at Eric while the one next to him just grunts. "We've lost five of ours so far, two still missing. You wouldn't happen to know anything about why that is, would you?"

"He had a bad day at the office?" Shrugging a shoulder nonchalantly, Eric shifts so he is between me and the abominations when I stop next to him.

It pisses me off, but I bite my tongue since I have no idea what is going on. His movement doesn't go unnoticed by the demons either. I can feel their eyes burning holes as they give me their full attention. *Great job, monster boy.*

"The word is that he's looking for someone." Abaddon, obviously the spokesperson for the grumpy duo, doesn't take his eyes off me.

Eric stiffens but his voice sounds bored, as if this whole conversation annoys him. "He is looking for some fun hunting, as usual. Or have you forgotten what happens when the Archangel gets bored?"

"This is different!" Abaddon snaps, and my hands grip the guns on instinct. His red eyes fall to my hands, and they start glowing. My gut feeling almost doubles me over from the evil he blasts my way. Glaring at Eric, he shoves an accusing finger at me. "He's looking for her!"

"I wouldn't do that if I were you." Eric's words are so calm and soft that even my self-preservation kicks in, and I have to wrestle with my fight or flight instinct.

The demon standing across from me strikes like a snake. His tree-trunk arm shoots towards me. I twist my body behind Eric's back to stay out of his reach. A crack of bone and a deafening howl from the demon rips through the silence before I stop my momentum. My guns are out and pointed in their faces as I stop on the other side of Eric, directly in front of Abaddon. From the corner of my eye, I see Eric still holding the arm of the now-quiet demon. His elbow bends in the wrong direction and a bone sticks out of his dark skin.

"I said, 'I wouldn't do that,'" Eric tells him conversationally, releasing the limb.

"She's a hunter!" Abaddon gives me a glance full of menace, and for the first time in twenty-four hours, a smile stretches my lips.

"Oh my God! She is!" I gush at him, blinking as if I can't believe it either. "Ah, ah, ah! Don't even twitch or I'll blow your brains out."

Eric chuckles next to me, and my stomach does a somersault at his husky laugh.

"What is the meaning of this, Shadow!" Abaddon doesn't look away from me.

"I need to know the word that's going around. I have no time to waste." Eric glares back, his green eyes turning amber, but I don't find that repulsive anymore. *Man, I'm screwed!*

"You promised last week that we would get to take care of our own and they'd leave us alone!" Abaddon spits angrily. "We trusted you and look where that got us!"

"I don't need your trust, or your loyalty," Eric barks, making the large demon take a step back while the other cowers, cradling his arm. "Speak!"

"They say he is looking for one of theirs that was taken. He claims we have started a new war, but he will finish it...starting with whoever has the hunter." Abaddon's eyes flick towards me. "We should give her back."

"*We* are not doing shit! You, on the other hand, are hiding something."

Abaddon focuses on Eric's clenched fists. "None of them are worth dying for. Not even if she was an Archangel herself!" Grinding his teeth, he barely squeezes the words out.

"That's not for you to decide. What else?"

"He promises freedom to live in this realm without

being hunted for whoever returns the hunter," Abaddon confesses begrudgingly.

"And where was he last seen?" My head turns to Eric, his tone pooling dread in my stomach.

Abaddon finally smiles, revealing a mouth full of white, razor-sharp teeth. "I love freedom to do as I please more than anything."

My gut feeling intensifies, alarms blaring in my head. How could we be so stupid? This situation has screamed trap from the moment we stopped the car, but as numb as I had been, I didn't pay attention at all. Without thinking, I pull a trigger. It takes Abaddon a second to realize that there is a bullet between his eyebrows. Black blood trickles down his nose as his eyes widen in disbelief. Eric grabs my arm, yanking me with him just as Abaddon keels over like a felled tree.

"Hel, run!"

Chapter Twenty - One

*E*lite hunters pour out from all sides. Eric doesn't let go of my hand as he bolts towards the car so fast I'm not sure if my feet are touching the ground or if I'm being pulled behind him like a kite. He skids to a halt a few feet away from the Porsche, and I body slam into his back, knocking all the air out of my lungs. My hands tighten on the guns as black spots dance in my eyes for a split second before his arm tugs me close to him. Knowing too well how hunters have no problem killing me on the spot, I spin so that my back is pressed to Eric's and pull his palm flat over my lower belly.

What an inappropriate time for warmth to gather

between my thighs and butterflies to flutter in my stomach. As if sensing my raging hormones, Eric's fingers flex, and he tightens his hold. Looking around, I count thirty, maybe forty hunters. They all stand ready, weapons of choice drawn, but none of them move. It's as if they are waiting to see what we will do.

"Hand her over, Eric. There is nowhere for you to go. You are surrounded," Michael's voice echoes, calm and smooth as silk, making me want to scream. He must be the reason why Eric stops so abruptly, but I couldn't see him through Eric's broad back and shoulders.

"She's not going anywhere," Eric states, his voice equally calm. I feel like a juicy bone between two hungry dogs. Anger, pain, and as much as I hate to admit, fear bubble up until it feels as if my skin needs to split open so the emotions can pour out.

"Enough!" my voice booms, making even me wince from the volume. "That's fucking enough!" Wiggling to get out of Eric's tight grip, I stumble when he removes his arm from around my waist.

"Language!" Michael snaps as I finally see him standing twenty feet in front of us, the car the only thing separating us.

"Really?" I deadpan, as my breathing speeds up from my anger. "Me saying fuck is what bothers you in this whole situation? Because from where I'm standing, the one saying fuck doesn't go around trying to kill innocent people!"

Eric growls next to me but says nothing.

"Who we are, what we say, do, don't do…that is what separates us from them!" Michael spits the word "them" as if he can't think of anything fouler.

"Them who?" My eyebrows go up as his eyes narrow. In the darkness, his angelic glow is like looking at the brightest star in the sky. "Them, as in the abominations who look grotesque and don't speak? Or them, the ones who look human and talk?" In my anger I gesture wildly with one of my guns. "Because until a week ago, none of us knew the talking ones existed! Or did that insignificant detail slip everyone's minds, oh holy one?" There are a few murmurs around us and the shuffling of feet, but I'm not sure if it's because of what I said, or if they are making sure I'm a locked target.

"Stop this charade, Helena! Step away from Eric and come with me." Lifting one hand, Michael gestures for me to go to him, and I narrow my eyes. "Or we can kill him and then you'll come with me." Shrugging, he drops his arm.

"And I'm to stay quiet and see how this plays out?" Crossing his arms, Eric sneers at the Archangel. My head snaps in his direction. "Because I was wrong. You don't want her dead, or she would've been five minutes ago."

My heart speeds up at his words and hope blooms in my chest. Did they realize they made a mistake? Can I go back now? As those questions spring in my mind, my gut tightens. If I believe Eric, these people have been trying to get rid of me for over a week. But what if he is trying to trick me? Dizziness makes me sway on my feet as my mind spins. A warm hand wraps around my arm. It's like an anchor to reality, stopping the spinning and calming me down. When I look up, not realizing I've been staring at the ground, my eyes lock on dark green ones full of concern and other things I'm not willing to acknowledge.

"I will not let them harm you. You have my word." Eric's words are softly spoken, for my ears only, and God or whoever listens help me, but I believe him.

"I don't have all night!" Michael snaps, making my hackles rise.

"I'm not going anywhere with you." My voice is low. Eric frowns before the pressure of his fingers on my arm decreases. Hurt flashes in his eyes, so subtle that if my eyes hadn't been on his I would have missed it.

Placing my hand, gun and all, over his to stop him from releasing me, I speak louder, not looking away from him. "Did you hear me, Archangel? I said, 'I'm not going anywhere with you!'" Heat burns in Eric's eyes and his fingers tighten around my arm.

"I don't think you have an option!" Michael growls and takes a step towards us.

"Hel, Run!" George's voice booms from behind me, but I don't have time to turn around to see him.

An explosion shakes the ground. Everyone staggers, some dropping to their knees, while those closest to it go air-born, their bodies flinging like dolls in the air and landing somewhere behind Michael. Eric doesn't miss a beat, throwing both of us towards the car and shoving me inside so fast I have no idea how he manages to even open the door. He disappears before I even sit up straight, and in one more blink he is sitting in the driver's seat.

"Buckle up!" he tells me through clenched teeth as he revs the engine and steps on the gas.

I ignore his words, already opening the window as fast as the electronic button will allow me. When the Porsche swerves in half a circle, I aim my gun. Michael is already in motion. The blast must have pushed him back since he's lifting himself off the ground, or he would've reached us already. Once standing, he lowers his head like a raging bull, his eyes blazing like liquid silver and his angelic face twisting in anger. Ignoring all the weapons flying towards us and clenching his fists, he sprints towards the car.

My hand is steady as I aim. My heartbeat slows down, and everything around me blurs and disappears into shadows. The only thing I can see is the majestic and magnificent Archangel coming full speed towards me, not blinking an eye at the gun I have aimed at his face. Michael's eyes are locked on mine, showing me every ounce of determination behind his gaze. He will never stop hunting me, regardless of the fact that I follow orders and do nothing but the right thing. In his eyes, I need to be removed. Just like the rest of us in the Order, he doesn't question his beliefs. I'm not like the rest of them, so like a virus, I need to be eliminated. My finger tightens on the trigger, but my entire being rebels against the very idea of trying to harm him. The jerk knows it too because a malicious smile lifts the corners of his lips. Cold sweat drenches my body from the look on his face.

Eric reaches over me, grabs my arm, and yanks it inside the car. My finger tightens instinctively, but the bullet goes wide, missing the Archangel a second before his body slams into my side of the vehicle, sending us spinning like some crazy carousel ride. Gripping the door handle, I hold onto it for dear life, but I shouldn't have worried. Eric has his arm over my chest, securing me to my seat better than any seatbelt. His other hand grips the steering wheel so hard I pray he doesn't rip it off. There is a look of purpose on his face, and his eyes are amber again, making his handsome face so drool-worthy that I forget to be afraid. All I can think about is how much I want to kiss him and remove the frown pulling his eyebrows down. As if sensing my intentions, his eyes jerk to my face. Hunger blazes in them as we stop spinning. The car rocks from side to side before stopping entirely. I open my mouth to say something to Eric, but my door gets ripped off the hinges with a screech that makes me shrink in the leather seat. Michael's arm reaches for me, trying to grab hold of my jacket, but the next second it disappears.

"Get out of here!" George screams, and I see it is him tackling Michael, giving me a chance. My chest contracts in gratitude before Eric steps on the gas again, and the Porsche flies into the night, leaving clouds of dust in our wake.

Chapter Twenty - Two

*M*ost of the drive back, I cling to the leather seat, making sure I don't fly out the gaping hole where the door used to be. Eric drives so fast I expect Michael to be right behind us, which is not the case. My heart is still in my throat from my inability to pull the trigger when my life is on the line. Worry about George eats a hole in my stomach. Through it all, Eric stays quiet, his eyes flicking from green to amber and back while he grips the steering wheel as if he's trying to strangle it.

I expect us to go to his apartment, or even Maddison's office, so I'm dumbfounded when he turns towards the bad neighborhoods of Atlanta. The tall buildings, cute storefronts, and manicured lawns of the cookie-cutter homes are replaced by run-down buildings. There are cardboards stuck to the windows, yellow grass is shriveling sparsely on the front yards that are looking more like junkyards, and cars with no wheels are scattered, propped up on bricks parked on the sides of the road. Slowing down, Eric pulls out a cell phone and types fast without looking. I watch his every move from the corner of my eye, not daring to look away from where we are going. I feel like if I look away for even a second, we will crash into something.

Without slowing too much, the Porsche swerves and we are instantly parked between the shell of an old Toyota and a rusted red pickup truck with a white door. Eric doesn't speak, so neither do I. Looking warily around, I try to see if we are here to hunt or hide. It does look like an area where abominations have been running rampant for a while.

"No demons here," Eric says as if reading my mind. I look at him thoroughly for the first time since we bolted out of that damn parking lot.

"Why are we here?"

My words are forgotten when a black SUV comes to a screeching halt next to us. Eric doesn't wait or explain. He jumps out of the car, comes to my side, and picks me up before I have a chance to voice a protest. The back door of the SUV opens as he takes two strides towards it, cradling me to his chest like I'm a child and my feet can't hold my weight. Setting me inside, his arms tighten around me as if he is reluctant to let me go before he straightens and heads to the other side. He slips in the back seat next to me, and the car takes off.

"Did you call Maddison?" Eric asks the guy driving.

"She said she will come to your place as soon as she's done fishing," a gravelly voice answers but I can't see the driver because of the panel separating the front and back seats.

"She's fishing?" I know it's absurd, and probably a code for something, but I ask anyway. Eric turns towards me and looks like he can't figure out if he knows me or not. His chest keeps rising and falling like the adrenaline is still coursing through him, so when he says nothing, I keep my mouth shut too. Looking out the window, I pay attention to where we are headed, noting names of streets. I shouldn't have bothered because before I know it, the SUV stops in front of Eric's building and he jumps out before we fully stop. I scramble after him, and right timing too because he opens the door and reaches for me. My feet are already touching the sidewalk when we look at each other from opposite sides of the car. His eyes narrow and my stomach clenches in response.

Slamming the door, he rounds the car with determined steps. Grabbing my hand, he pulls me with him. He is taller than me, so I have to almost jog to keep up. He has a death grip on my hand, and if I trip, he'll probably drag me behind him. The security guy behind his corner station smiles politely as he lifts his shiny bald head but ducks it down as soon as he sees Eric's expression. I can only imagine how we look.

Luckily, the elevator doors are open, or in his mood, Eric would probably have climbed the stairs all the way to the top floor rather than wait. As soon as we are inside, he jams his finger forcefully on the button, and we shoot up to his apartment. He still holds my hand, and I don't pull it away. After everything, I feel so cold inside that I don't think I'll ever feel the fire inside me again, so his warm hand is a beautiful distraction. His thumb glides back and forth on the back of my hand, but we reach the top before I can overthink all the reasons why this is a bad idea.

When we walk inside, he drops my hand and takes a couple of longer strides to distance himself. My feet slow down and I stop a couple of steps inside the front door. Eric's shoulders lift and fall like he is fighting for breath, and his hands clench at his sides. Swallowing all my remarks and smart-ass comments, I wait him out. From the first moment I saw him, he has never appeared winded or tired. Even when upset in Maddison's office, his body didn't look like granite, coiled up, ready to snap and destroy everything around him. That's exactly how he looks now. Without meaning to, my feet take me to him, and I gently place my hand on his back. He stiffens even more, if that is possible. He doesn't even appear to be breathing now.

"You okay?" Keeping my voice calm, I move my hand

gently from side to side, remembering that Maddison asked how I knew my touch would calm him down. "Is there anything I can do to help?"

"He almost took you tonight." His voice is much deeper and more guttural than usual. Goosebumps cover me from head to toe.

"But he didn't."

"He didn't thanks to that hunter, not thanks to me!" He snarls, turning his head, but he doesn't look at me, only carries on staring into the distance while giving me a perfect view of his profile.

"Come on, Eric. George couldn't have done anything on his own." My stomach clenches in worry for my friend. "And does it even matter? We got away, which is a lot more than my friend can say." My voice breaks, and Eric whirls on me.

"I had to get you away; I couldn't stop for him."

My head lifts so I can keep eye contact with him. He presses so close that my breasts get crushed to his chest. There is guilt in his eyes.

"Are you sure you are a demon?" I whisper as his handsome face looks down on me.

"Would you like me if I wasn't? Would you have trusted me, my word?" His green eyes search mine and guilt pierces my heart at the vulnerability I see.

"I do like you." I'm not even sure I spoke out loud until his nostrils flare again as if he is scenting the air. "You can smell it if I don't tell the truth!" Trying to take a step away from him doesn't work well. His arms wrap around me, crushing me to his chest.

"I can." Eric doesn't look away, daring me to call him an abomination, even bracing himself for it.

I surprise us both by saying, "I like you a lot, actually."

"But you don't trust me."

"Trust is not given, monster boy. Trust is earned."

"I can work with that." The lustful smile that lifts his lips almost makes my knees buckle.

Chapter Twenty-Three

We stand barely inside his apartment with the front door still open, as if suspended in time. He radiates heat, and my bone-deep chill draws me impossibly closer to him. Eric holds me captive with his penetrating gaze, and I'm powerless to look away or move. My heart hammers in my chest, but I'm hoping he doesn't notice. I'm not comfortable knowing he is aware of how his nearness affects me until I feel his heartbeat match mine. Slowly, my gaze shifts from his handsome face to his neck. There, on the side, a vein betrays his calm facade by pulsing wildly, matching the throb between my thighs.

Eric's nostrils flare again, and I press my thighs together, horrified at the idea that he can somehow smell my desire. My face heats. Ducking my head, I press my forehead under his chin, hiding like an immature girl. He chuckles, and the vibration of his deep voice makes me shiver involuntarily. I expect him to kiss me by now, but he just keeps staring at me, and I fear that maybe I'm reading him wrong.

"You're cold." Unwrapping his arms from around me, he rubs his hands up and down my arms. "Let's get you warmed up."

He steps away, closing and locking the door before leading me through the large living room. Like the rest of his place, the room is done in all dark colors. Black leather couches are placed around a white marble coffee table, facing a wall with a theater-style screen instead of a TV. Abstract paintings of female torsos in shades of red and orange are the only color in the entire place. A wall-to-floor window covers a whole side, giving me the view of Atlanta. I imagine him sitting here staring at his domain like the king of the world.

Eric opens the door to his bedroom and pulls me straight towards the bathroom. I don't protest, curiosity getting the better of me. Earlier in the day, he let me use his guest bathroom to freshen up. I want to see how his personal space differs, so my feet follow him without question. When he flicks on the light, my jaw hits the glossy floor tiles. It's like stepping through time to a bathing chamber in some ancient temple. The sink looks like it's been carved from rock with the faucet hidden under what looks like real flowers draping low from the wall above it. An open shower stands in the left corner, water running from the wall like an indoor fountain. But it's the built-in pool that can easily fit ten people in it taking most of the space up that has me frozen. One side of it ends with a full wall window overlooking the city. All I can do is stare as my feet take me further inside the stunning bathroom.

"I take it you like the view?"

Turning around to look at him, my breath catches in my throat.

He is leaning one shoulder on the doorframe, arms crossed over his chest. The lighting makes his green eyes sparkle as he watches my reaction, and I can't help the slight smile I aim his way. His five 'o'clock shadow makes him more roguishly handsome, while pieces of his hair fall all around his face where it escapes the band he has it tied back in.

"That's the understatement of the year. Its breathtaking"

He chuckles and pushes off the door, stepping towards me. "I can't say that I agree." Stopping in front of me, he tugs on my jacket, and I let him remove it.

"You don't think this view is priceless and

breathtaking?" Both my eyebrows go up as I look at him like I'm evaluating his sanity. Throwing his head back, he laughs, and I gape at him like a dumbstruck, lovesick fool.

"I didn't say it's not good," he says when he stops laughing. "I'm just saying I have a view of something else that takes my breath away." Taking hold of my t-shirt, he slowly pulls it up, as if expecting me to protest. I'm beyond the point of no return, so I lift my arms up.

"Cheesy, monster boy." I roll my eyes, pretending I'm offended, and he chuckles again. I love that sound.

"Truth, cupcake." He winks and grins when I scowl at him for his use of that nickname.

"Okay, fine! I won't call you monster boy anymore. Just stop using that horrible nickname."

"I'll think about it." He chuckles and ducks out of the way when I swipe at him.

Catching my outstretched arm, he pulls me to him and grabs my hips to hold me there. This whole game of tug-o-war is fraying my nerves, so as soon the skin of his arms connects with my bare skin, I reach up and bury my hands in his hair. His eyes widen before I pull his head down and kiss him like I have never kissed anyone in my life. He stiffens when my lips touch his for a split second. I almost pull away, but he recovers quickly, and his tongue invades my mouth without hesitation.

Eric devours my mouth with deep grunts of satisfaction echoing and bouncing off the bathroom tiles. My moans join him a moment later, while he guides me backward until I feel the rock sink press against the back of my thighs. His hands glide over my ass and grip me just below it as he lifts me up and places me on the stone.

Leaving my mouth, he trails kisses up and down my neck, licking, sucking, and biting gently over every exposed service there before his hand takes hold of my red, lacy bra. He pulls the cup down until my breast pops free. His lips latch onto my nipple, lashing it with his tongue, while he pinches my other nipple through the lace. Bracing one hand on the rock beneath me for the sake of my sanity, I grab a fistful of Eric's hair, holding him to me as if he is trying to escape. He lifts his head and kisses me roughly again as he wedges his hips between my legs and grinds his erection on my throbbing core. Both of us moan, long and loud. We both fumble with belts and zippers before I push his leather pants low on his hips. His rock-hard cock pulses in my hand. Eric shoves his hand none too gently inside my panties, and groans when his fingers get drenched. Our hips slowly gyrate in sync as we use the same air to breathe and chase the tightening band inside both of us to a snapping point. He pulls his lips away, breathing hard, clenching his jaw as he stares intently at my face.

"I need you to cum for me now, Hel. Do it so I can fuck you until you pass out on me." My heart beats faster at his rough words and the hunger in his eyes. His fingers keep up the fast tempo of pumping into me, first two, then a third. The heel of his palm grinds on my button, sending tiny electric shocks through my body.

"No!" Grinding my teeth, I cling onto this feeling that I don't want to end. Eric grins devilishly at me before he twists his hand, making his thumb press just right on my clit. I explode.

My muscles clamp around his fingers, holding there and trying to suck him deeper inside with each pulsing tremor. My whole body shakes like I've received an electric shock while he holds me to him, making as much noise as I am, as if my orgasm feels as good to him as it does to me. Lights flash behind my closed eyelids, and I shamelessly scream his name. When I finally calm down, Eric buries his face in my hair, hugging me tightly as he whispers my name. His fingers are still inside me, so I reach for his cock again, but the blaring song of his cell phone makes us both groan. Eric fishes it out of his pocket, lifting it to his ear.

"Yes!" he snaps at whoever is on the other side. "Okay!" Putting his phone in his pocket, he scrubs that hand over his face. "Maddison is here."

"What?" I screech, scrambling to push him away and dress. "She heard everything?" I look at him, mortified when he doesn't move away.

"She's downstairs, coming up now." He chuckles as he reluctantly pulls his fingers out of me, making me moan. "And don't worry, Hel. We are going to finish this later." With those words, he sucks his fingers into his mouth, licking them clean before winking and sauntering out of the bathroom with his pants barely hanging on his hips. All I can do is stare after him while my insides pulse with a desire to call him back and make him keep his promise.

Chapter Twenty-Four

Maddison is sitting primly on one of the leather couches in the living room by the time I shower and calm myself down from the whirlwind of emotions Eric stirred up inside me. I was grateful to find a pair of sweatpants and a t-shirt waiting for me when I exited the bathroom. I had to roll the legs up a few times, and the t-shirt is almost mid-thigh, but they are clean, and I feel like a newborn. As soon as I step into the living room, their conversation stops. My eyes narrow.

"Don't stop on my account. Or is it something I'm not supposed to know?" Stomping up to the couch opposite Maddison, I curl my feet under me and sink into the soft leather.

"Not everyone is hiding things from you, Hel." Eric sounds tired, and he scrubs a hand over his face.

"Could've fooled me," I mumble, ignoring his sharp gaze. "Maddison, nice to see you again."

"I heard what happened." She cuts to the chase, and I'm grateful.

"Yeah, one clusterfuck after another. Just another day in the life of Helena." I can't hide the bitterness in my voice.

"As much as I would like to tell you anything to make you feel better, I would have to agree." Maddison lifts a hand, stopping Eric from talking. "You are not a child who needs to be sheltered from the truth. It seems Michael will stop at nothing to get to you, including making deals with Abaddon." She gives Eric a peculiar look, and he scowls at her.

"Abaddon is an idiot!" he calls out, then he paces the length of the room. "That moron almost got her captured. Useful, or not, keep him away from me, Maddison. I'll kill the fucker next time I see him."

"Anyone like to share some details so I know what is going on? How does Abaddon fit into all this?"

Eric clenches his jaw and his fists, but Maddison has a calculating look in her bright blue eyes.

"Abaddon and his twin were given to me by my mother when I decided to live in this realm. Humans would call them bodyguards," she says, lacing her fingers over her knee.

"To keep you safe from the Order and the hunters?" Curiosity gets the better of me, and I'm intrigued by their world now that I know not all of them are human-eating abominations.

"Among other things, yes." She smiles, and I can't help but stare at how beautiful she is. Her eyes glow slightly, and the green color of her shirtdress make her red hair look like flames around her face. "Humans, too."

"I'm sorry, what?" I blink stupidly at her.

"To keep me safe from humans, as well." Peals of feminine laughter surround me when I only blink again at that. "Oh, Helena. You think only demons can do evil things? Come now, you cannot be that naïve."

"What can a human possibly do to a demon? You are stronger, faster, and a supernatural being no matter how fragile you look." Eric grimaces at my words, and I sneer at him. "Tell me it's not true!" I snap, and he clears his face of any expression.

"That is true, but just because I am stronger doesn't mean I want to go around hurting them," Maddison answers, also staring daggers at Eric. "Let her ask her questions. Why does it bother you that she doesn't believe some things? If she told you her perspective of the Order, would you believe her, or would you start arguing your point of view?"

"What is it with you women? I said nothing!" Crossing his arms, he scowls at both of us.

"You don't have to say anything; your face said it all."

Tucking my hands between my knees, I look away from his penetrating green eyes.

"I need to make a phone call." He turns and goes to his bedroom mumbling about women and him never being able to do anything right. My eyes follow him, looking at his shoulders sway with every step.

"Don't mind him." My eyes meet Maddison's." He is afraid but doesn't want to show it."

"Afraid of Michael? I can't say I blame him. I never thought an angel could be more terrifying than a demon. Count me corrected in that regard." Maddison bursts out laughing again, and I gape at her. "I wasn't trying to be funny."

"He is not afraid of Michael." Placing her hand over her chest, she keeps laughing like I just told her the best joke of the century. After her laughter dies down, she gasps. "He is afraid of you."

"Of me?"

"Oh, you silly girl. Yes, you! If what you said is true, and you are half angel, half demon, it means you are the last of your kind in existence. Not just the Archangels, but all the Fallen, too, made sure every single one of you were killed. The Archangels killed them to keep the Fallen bound to Hell, and the demons killed them by bleeding them dry in hopes of opening the gates of Hell. And here you are, alive and causing trouble just by taking a breath. So, yes, he is afraid of what that all means to him, to all of us. But also, he is afraid because he will do anything to protect you, even if it kills him."

"I have done nothing to deserve his protection. Don't get me wrong, I'm grateful, but I don't want to cause more trouble than all of you already have. I'll figure it out. I will leave and…"

"Haven't you seen the way he is looking at you?" Maddison cuts me off, narrowing her eyes. "Are you that stupid, or are you blind?"

"You don't go around risking your life for someone you want to fuck, Maddison, so get off your high horse." Glaring at her, I fight to contain my anger. "I'll go away so he doesn't have to worry about any of you getting in more shit with that deranged Archangel."

"You really can't tell, can you? You don't even know who Eric is." She searches my eyes, but I don't know what she's hoping to find. "I thought since you were half demon you would simply know."

"Know what?" Tired, frustrated, and bone weary, I sigh heavily.

"That I am Lucifer's son, and I have claimed you as my own." My head snaps in his direction, and my jaw hits my chest.

Chapter Twenty - Five

"Oh, hell no!" Jumping from the couch, I move away from them both. "No way in hell anyone is claiming anything! And Lucifer? What the fuck?"

"Helena…"

"Don't you *Helena* me, you asshole! You forgot to mention that tiny bit of information before you shoved your hand in my pants!" Seething, I whirl on Eric, forgetting to even be embarrassed that Maddison is listening to all this.

"I think you should calm down…"

"Whatever possessed you to think it's smart to tell a pissed off woman to calm down is beyond me." Maddison huffs, cutting Eric off. A blast of hysterical laughter bursts out of my mouth.

"I must either be dead, or I'm in some sort of coma living out my nightmares while I'm trapped in my head!" I tell them both, deflating, all the anger leaving me so suddenly that I almost drop where I stand.

"Please, sit down," Maddison coaxes me while Eric stands frozen in place, glaring, and grinding his jaw so hard I can almost hear it. "Let's talk and clear things up once and for all."

"I'm not sure I want to hear more than what I already know." Grumbling, I force my feet back towards the couch because she does have a point. "And I don't mean that just about you." I twirl my hand in Eric's direction. "I'm saying in general, about everything. Angels, the Order, demons…all of it."

"It must not be easy to have everything dumped on you at once." Maddison's eyes soften, and my stomach clenches.

"I'm still kinda waiting to wake up," I tell no one in particular, sighing and rubbing a hand over my face.

"We have been here for centuries…us, but the angels as well," Maddison starts, not waiting on anyone to agree or ask questions. "At the beginning, it was brutal. The war lasted a very long time, but eventually, we all got tired of it. So we agreed to keep to ourselves and stay out of each other's way." Her eyes lose focus, as if she's lost in memories while Eric stiffly moves to sit next to her, avoiding my eyes. "With no war to keep us occupied, we started looking for trouble. We ended up having rogues, or abominations as you like to call them. But we were not the only ones. More angels fell too. We now patrol and clean up the problem before the humans notice. Sometimes we don't make it on time. There are only so many of us in our group. That's when the Order steps up. We do the same if we come across a fallen that's harming humans or threatening to expose us. We have been asking the Order to let us deal with our own forever. They don't stop at the rogues; They kill any demon on sight. Michael never agreed. Until last week, when the Order contacted Eric and made him the offer. Kill you in exchange for being free to police our own."

"And instead of killing me, he watched my back and saved my life." Guilt for everything I said earlier overwhelms me, but I swallow it down and keep as calm and collected as possible.

"I told you I couldn't do it. Not that I didn't come to find you to snuff out your life." Eric's cold detachment causes a lump to form in my throat.

"But you just told me that you are Lucifer's son. Wouldn't you want to help your father keep the gate open?"

"We don't see eye to eye on many things."

"What does that mean, Eric?" I search his eyes, but they are closed off, not letting me see anything. "I need things spoken clearly, not in riddles."

"It means he wants Lucifer away from humans more than Michael does," Maddison chirps.

"Why?" Honest curiosity pushes the question out, and I don't shy away. I let both of them see it clearly.

"Because after everything, Lucifer is bitter, and if he opens that gate, no human will be left alive after the first day. Ever since the fall, all he has been doing is looking for a way out. It drove him insane. Trust me! He is better kept where he is." Eric finally relaxes his shoulders, leaning back on the couch and closing his eyes.

Silence drapes like a heavy blanket, and we all sit lost in thought. My eyes flick restlessly from left to right, my mind racing with one idea after another. What they are telling me is the truth. They have no reason to lie. It's not like I'm a hostage that they're trying to convert. They've saved my life repeatedly—well Eric did—without asking anything in return. And then the truth hits me like a builder.

"And I am his ticket to Lucifer!" Wide-eyed, I look from Maddison's concerned face to Eric's determined one. "Michael wanted me dead at first, but he changed plans. He wants to use me to get to your father."

"They will not have you, Helena." Eric's voice is soft but holds such a promise of pain to whoever stands in his way that I physically shiver. "They can't have you. If you don't believe anything else I say, believe that."

"It's not just Michael looking for me, is it?" Their expressions give me the answer before they even speak.

"No, it's not. But that's not important right now." Maddison reaches over and squeezes Eric's shoulder gently. "We need to come up with a plan."

"A plan for what? To hide?" She's shaking her head before I even finish the sentence.

"To discover our allies. We already know the enemies." Determination sets on her face.

"Us? Are you crazy? You should stay as far away from me as possible. Obviously, I bring nothing but trouble."

"True, but you are a—"

"Let's go!" Not letting her finish, I jump from the couch and stride towards the door.

"And where are we going?" Eric is right on my heels, and I'm grateful he is not trying to stop me.

"To see if we can find the snake in the grass!" Jerking the door open, my unwavering steps are followed by Maddison's laughter.

"Oh, I like her more with every word she says!" she calls after us.

Chapter Twenty-Six

Okay, so going back to grab my guns killed my dramatic exit, but at least I feel better about having them with me. Eric asks no questions while my mind spins. That conversation with Maddison was like someone pulling the blindfold from my eyes. Why I didn't think of this before I have no idea. Michael could've killed me the second he set his sights on me, no matter who watched. Because I am half demon, they all would cheer him on. Well, maybe not Hector, but the verdict on that one is still pending. Yet, he spends his time talking, strutting around with his wings on full display like a peacock, talking nonsense. No, he isn't going to kill me. Hurt me? I don't doubt that anymore, but he wants to keep me alive and use me to get to Lucifer. A shiver runs up my spine.

"Why did you stop me from shooting Michael?" Turning towards Eric, his profile glows from the passing lights of the city as he drives the black SUV that has been stolen for my crazy plan.

"You were going to regret pulling the trigger," he says it so matter-of-fact that my eyes narrow.

"How would you know what I'd regret? He was trying to kill us!" Okay, so I'm angry at everything and I'm taking it out on him, but it's not like he doesn't deserve it.

"You hesitated. That's all I needed to know." Turning his head, his green eyes lock on mine, and I see how much my tantrum has hurt him.

I don't know how, or why for that matter, but I can read him so easily. Maybe he is allowing me to see what he's feeling, I'm not sure. One thing I know is, seeing that I've hurt him when all he has ever done is helped me makes me feel like someone has reached inside my chest, grabbed hold of my heart and is squeezing it as hard as they can. While people I've trusted stab me in the back and do their best to make sure I'm dead or captured, I'm lashing out at those who stand by my side, when anyone in their right mind would turn and run screaming.

"I'm sorry." Not looking away from him, I put as much sincerity as possible into my words. His gaze flicks to mine for a second before he takes a sharp turn and parks on the side of the road.

"You really mean that?" Eric looks at me with so much intensity a shiver runs up and down my spine.

"Of course I mean it." Looking away, I scrub a hand over my face in frustration. "I know I've been acting like an idiot since you've met me." Lifting a hand, I stop whatever he was about to say. "No need for pretty little lies so we can protect the fragile little girl, monster boy. I was acting like an idiot, and I will freely admit it. I wasn't joking when I said this whole thing seems like a nightmare that I'm waiting to wake up from."

"That's understandable." Eric's soft words make me look at him again.

"Maybe." A humorless smile tilts my lips. "It still doesn't mean it's right."

"And who's to say what's right or wrong, Hel?"

"I don't know. We should ask Michael." This time, a real, albeit small, smile shows on my face, but I sober up immediately. "Anyway…what I'm trying to say is, I'm really sorry for lashing out at you. Everything that happened in the last week or so has to come out in some way. I'm letting it out the wrong way by taking it out on you and acting like a two-year-old who needs help figuring things out. The situation is what it is. I can't change who I am or who my parents are any more then you can change who your father is. Why should I be different, but hold that against you? You have done nothing to prove that I have grounds to be distrustful or hateful towards you specifically."

"They do say the devil is in the details." A small smile tugs at his lips and my heart clenches at the sad look in his eyes.

"From where I'm sitting, the devil is right across from me. And he is not good for my sanity."

"If it makes you feel better, you're not good for his sanity either." The crooked smile he gives me speeds up my heartbeat, and I cup his face. He nuzzles in my palm almost as if he can't help himself.

"It's good to know that, so I don't feel like a school girl with a crush on the bad boy."

"I wasn't joking, nor did I have a different agenda when I said they couldn't have you, Helena." The hairs on the back of my neck stand at attention when Eric's eyes flash amber. "You might need time to trust me, or whatever it is you women need. All that is fine with me. But know one thing for sure: You are mine, and whoever wants to get to you will have to go through me first."

"Aww, my knight in—"

Eric cuts off my smartass remark when he tugs me towards him, his mouth devouring mine in only an instant. It's not the gentle kiss that would've been appropriate after the promise he made. His soft lips crash on mine, and his tongue pushes its way inside my mouth, tangling with mine in an all-consuming kiss. My heart thunders as I grip his arms. Everything going through my head vanishes into nothingness. One of Eric's hands wraps in my hair at the back of my head, and he uses it to angle me any way he wants while the other is around my waist pulling me over to his lap. My legs and knees bump into things, sending little pings of pain through me, but I manage to follow his lead and straddle him in the driver's seat without pulling back for air. At the moment I think breathing is overrated anyway. Especially when my pulsing core settles on his hard shaft and his hips jerk up, pressing even harder where I need him most.

I'm still wearing his sweatpants and t-shirt, so his hand slips easily inside the waistband, and his sizeable, calloused hand grabs hold of my ass, pulling me impossibly closer to him. A deep, painful groan rumbles from his chest when his hand touches only bare skin rather than panties. Another wave of heat pulls in my lower belly at the sound, and my hips move on their own when his fingers delve between my folds. Pulling on my hair, he un-fuses our lips and starts frantically kissing and nipping down my neck.

"You are driving me insane," Eric growls, sounding like he might rip something apart at any moment, and a shiver rakes my body.

Without thinking, I push my upper body away from him, trying to give him access to my aching breasts. My back collides with the steering wheel and the blaring sound of the horn scares the crap out of me. His arms wrap around me, pulling me towards him, and his body stiffens for a second before we slowly turn to look at each other. We both burst out laughing at the absurdity of the moment. Eric is still holding me in his embrace as we keep gasping for air.

"Beware of the horn monster!" I manage between laughs. Eric just shakes his head and chuckles more while one of his hands slowly rubs up and down my back.

"It's nice to see you laugh, Hel," he says softly after our laughter dies down. I just smile at him. "Now, where exactly are we going?" That question reminds me that I never told him where we were headed.

"If you didn't know, then where were you driving us to?" Snickering, I crawl out of his lap and settle back in the passenger seat. He lets me go reluctantly, his hands still lingering on my body.

"Nowhere in particular. I figured you'd tell me eventually." Smiling sheepishly, he shrugs. Looking at him, I can't help thinking, *And this is the evil they want us to kill?*

"I need to go to the sanctuary." He stiffens. "Not go inside. I'm not stupid. I just want to watch the comings and goings for a while."

"Okay. Let's go stalk us some hunters then." Relaxing, he grins, starts the SUV, and peels off the side of the road.

Chapter Twenty-Seven

We park about a block away from the sanctuary. The building is outside the city of Atlanta on a big piece of land with a lot of space for obstacle courses, training grounds, and other amenities that the Founders thought necessary for us hunters. All those things are behind the monstrosity of a building that for all intents and purposes looks like an ancient cathedral to the unassuming humans. Green lawns and trees surround it, creating a picture of pristine peace and serenity. The private dirt road leading towards it cuts through a small planted wood, giving us enough cover to silently stalk towards it. This place where I'm headed like some thief dressed in too-large, dark clothing is the place I used to call home. My safe haven. But not anymore…now, it's where my family plans my demise.

My heart rate picks up the closer we get, and as if he can hear it, Eric presses close enough that I can feel his body heat at my back. As a hunter, it should bother me to have someone so close behind me, but his presence has a calming effect. The annoyance I expect is missing, and it gets me a little worried. I should be more on guard with everyone and their brother after me. Luckily, I can see the sanctuary through the trees, and I have no time to overthink things.

Stopping, I look over my shoulder at Eric. My breath catches in my throat when his face is so close to me I can almost feel his breath tickling my lips. Pulling back, he looks at me intently. I blink a couple of times before my brain catches up with why I stopped. His lips twitch at my stupefied gawking, and that's enough to snap me out of the daze. I used to think girls were stupid for drooling over guys, and here I am doing the same at the worst possible moment in my life. *Get your head in the game Hel!* I yell internally, before pointing my hand and indicating that Eric should move to the opposite side of the dirt road so we cover more ground. I don't want any surprises today, and hunters patrol these grounds. Hell, I used to patrol them after I turned eighteen. Eric nods sharply once and gives me a quick kiss on the lips before slinking away through the trees like a shadow. Which reminds me, he never told me why Abaddon calls him Shadow, but that has to wait for now.

Pressing my body close to the large tree trunk I picked as my hiding spot, I get as comfortable as possible for the long wait by leaning my body against the tree. The night will be coming to an end soon enough. If my senses are correct, we have a maximum of a few hours before it will be too light to stick around. The sanctuary is busiest at night, and just like nothing has changed—apart from my life going to shit—teams go in and out through the front yard.

After an hour of watching the same thing over and over, the activity picks up a notch. Twisting my blonde hair in a knot, I shove it inside the collar of the t-shirt so it doesn't get in my face every time I lean on the side of the tree. Squinting, I try to see the faces of those coming and going, and I'm surprised to see strangers instead of the hunters I've known my entire life. That can't be good for me if they've called other teams here. Or it might not have anything to do with me and more to do with the increase of abominations everywhere. I guess we will never know.

The crack of a branch breaking makes my entire body freeze, and my ears strain. The area around me gets unusually quiet, and I slowly turn around, pressing my back to the tree so I have a better view of the little forest. I'm hoping it's just Eric getting bored of the lurking-like-creeps game and coming to tell me we should return another night. Even as I think that, I know it's not him because if that man has anything in spades, it's patience. Gripping my guns tighter, I examine my surroundings, careful not to miss even the slight movement of a leaf. Nothing stirs, and no sound comes from the trees, so after a couple of minutes, I give up staring.

When I turn back around, the front of the Sanctuary is all empty, as if there weren't a few dozen hunters strutting about earlier. The only people I can see are the poor suckers who ended up on guard duty moving purposely around the building from opposite sides. From where I am, I finally see that guard duty is really a punishment. It would be so easy for me to slip inside the sanctuary with only those four around. It's almost as if the Order is giving the middle finger to those like Eric or me now, saying "We have no protection at the moment, but you can't do shit about it." It pisses me off immensely, and I can only imagine how that feels to Eric, or Maddison, if they've had to deal with this for however long it's been going on.

Deciding not to think about it anymore so I don't get more upset, I drape my body on the tree trunk, almost hugging it, and keep watching the four guards do their rounds. The rumbling sound of a vehicle breaks the silence, making me drop on all fours and crawl around the tree so the headlights don't give me away when it drives past. After a minute a black SUV that looks a lot like the one in front of Maddison's office and the one we used to drive here, comes rolling towards the front of the building, stopping almost at the steps of the front door. It's different from the ones the Order uses, but only when you look at the wheels. The rims are much larger, and the tires look more fitting for a tank than an urban vehicle.

Holding my breath, I scramble to lift myself up in hopes I'll see who is in it. The night is almost at an end, and it's not pitch black anymore. It's some muted color of gray where it can't decide if it should stay as night or let the new day start. My heart stops, and my entire body stiffens when a body presses me between firm muscles and the tree, while a hand wraps around my mouth, cutting off the terrified shriek that is ready to burst out. I didn't hear a sound to alert me that someone was that close. My brain kicks into gear, realizing how stupid it would've been if I scream while hiding. I jerk my hips as hard as I can into the groin of whoever is holding me captive. My hand lifts up, and I use my gun to hit the asshole's head over my shoulder. The thumping sound is like music to my ears. As soon as his grip on my mouth loosens, I bite his hand as hard as I can, almost drawing blood. The groan of pain makes me all giddy. Well, it makes me giddy until he speaks.

"Damn it, woman, stop hitting me," Eric growls quietly as he cradles his head in his hand while holding the one I bit pressed to his groin. I bite my lips to stop the laughter that wants to come out and his eyes narrow.

"We missed seeing who was in that SUV." I point out to stop whatever he is going to say about the ninja moves

I just pulled on him. The laughter I'm suppressing is evident in my voice, and his eyes turn to slits.

"I know who was in it," Eric tells me before flicking his eyes over my shoulder towards the Sanctuary. Taking a breath, I'm about to ask who.

"As do I." The familiar voice coming from behind Eric cuts off any words that were going to pass my lips. Lifting my arm, I place it over Eric's shoulder, pointing the gun at the intruder's face.

Chapter Twenty-Eight

"I would prefer not to have a bullet in my head if you don't mind, Hel," Hector says tiredly, but I don't lower my arm. Eric twists around, stepping next to me to face Hector.

"What are you doing here?" I can't stop myself from barking the words at him.

"I could ask the same. I, on the other hand, live here, remember?" A small smile lifts Hector's lips, but it looks so sad that my gut clenches when I see it.

"I know where you live. Why are you out here, and not inside? And how many of you are around?" My gut feeling stays quiet, so I know no one means to attack. At least for now.

"It's just me." At my raised eyebrow, Hector huffs. "I knew you'd come back here eventually. I taught you everything you know. I've been checking this area since you left with him." He points his chin at Eric.

"He has a name and I know you know it," I point out, still glaring at him. I'm not angry, I'm hurt, damn it.

"Eric." Hector winces, then nods in acknowledgment when I call him out on his bullshit. "I'm guessing you told her everything."

"Hector." Eric's deep voice calms me a little. "No, not everything, but she knows the gist of it. We haven't had much time for talking, what with trying to keep her alive and out of Michael's hands." Subtle, Eric is not. I appreciate that about him.

While Eric talks, I look closely at Hector. The proud, elegant man that I've known my whole life is nowhere to be seen. His face looks drawn and his skin pale. More wrinkles have appeared, and dark circles puff up under his eyes. Even his hair looks mussed, like he's been running his hands through it too many times. His once-elegant robes are wrinkled, too, and it kills me to see him like this. He is the only close family I've ever had. If I didn't know better, I would think he is on the run, too.

"What's wrong with you?" I blurt out, and finally lower my gun.

"What do you mean?" A frown pulls Hector's eyebrows down and Eric turns to look at me.

"You look like you're on the run, too." Giving him a

once over again, I lock eyes with him. "What's wrong with you?"

"I'm an old man who has made too many mistakes in my life. What's not wrong with me?" His voice cracks, and my heart does the same. "What are you wearing?" he says, as if noticing my clothes for the first time. He frowns harder, making his face scrunch up.

"I had to run for my life so I couldn't pack. I had to wash up all the dirt and grime from when my own people tried to kill me. What else should I be wearing?" If I sound bitter, well, it's because I am.

"Wait a second," he mumbles and, turning around, he disappears between the trees.

Eric and I look at each other, and he shrugs at me as if saying, "Let's see what will happen." He's mostly quiet, but I'm not fooled. His body is coiled tight, ready to spring into action, and his nostrils flare as if scenting the air while his head tilts this way and that, listening for threats. His movements are so subtle and barely perceptive, but they are there. Ever since he kissed me, it's like I'm in tune with everything he does. I can even tell when his adrenaline starts rushing, making him ready to move fast. It's an unnerving feeling.

The rustling of feet over dried leaves and grass announces that Hector is back. We both turn at the same time to see the old man wrestling a large duffle bag, almost dragging it behind him. Without waiting, Eric walks up and takes it from him, dropping it with a thump where I'm still standing. I look at it as if it might bite me before I lift my eyes to Hector in question.

"As I said, I knew you'd come eventually, and you'd need some of your stuff." Shrugging his shoulder, he lowers his eyes as if embarrassed by the admission.

"Why the sudden change of heart?" Hector looks at me sharply. "Don't give me that fucking look!" I snap at him. "First you ask Eric to kill me. Then, so I don't get killed, you make sure my best friend is killed. Now you're helping me? Shit doesn't add up in your favor."

Eric takes a breath to say something, but I lift a hand, stopping whatever is about to come from him. Still glaring at Hector, I wait, not ready to let him brush off what he did as some sort of misunderstanding. Saying something wrong or doing something stupid is one thing. Trying to get someone to kill the one you've raised is a totally different matter. Crossing my arms awkwardly because I'm still holding my guns, I wait for his answer.

"I never wanted Eric to kill you." When I open my mouth, Hector narrows his gaze, shaking his head to keep me from talking. "I let you talk, now you will listen. I don't think I have much time." He waits until I nod before he nods in return, as if satisfied with my compliance. "I asked him to track you down to kill you, yes. Amanda is just another life from the long list I'll have to pay penance for. Everything I did was to ensure your survival, but that is my cross to bear, not yours. I had my reasons, and the most important was to be sure that Eric wouldn't do it if what I know about him is true. Do you think he would've agreed to come find you, and protect you, if I just walked up to him out of nowhere and told him that? Those are my hunters killing his kind every night, not just their rogues."

"Yet, you lied to us all, and like fools, we followed blindly, trusting every word coming out of your mouth," I spit the words at him. Eric just growls deep in his throat, clenching his fists so hard I can hear his bones cracking.

"I was raised in the Order just like you were. We all thought we were doing the right thing. When all the little details that make you start doubting things appear, there was always a good explanation for everything. An anomaly like sometimes you must sacrifice for the greater good and other such rubbish. After years pass you start turning a blind eye, or you wouldn't be able to live with yourself, not if you look too closely and admit that you've lived a lie, that you've done horrible things in the name of good, including hurting innocents while living that lie."

"If you're trying to make me feel sorry for you, I'm sorry to say that I can't find it in me at the moment," I say honestly. That gets me a proud smile from him.

"I wouldn't expect anything else from you, Helena. You have always made me proud, even when I didn't show it." Hector's words warm my insides, even though I'll never admit it to him. "As I was saying, me asking him to find you in a way that I knew he would agree to was the smartest thing I've ever done. You have this glow about you, this aura you project that makes everyone pay attention. I knew it'd intrigue him enough to observe you first. He did exactly what I prayed he would. And you are safe now, thank the Heavens."

"Your God or his Heavens have nothing to do with it, old man!" Eric growls, and goosebumps cover my arms.

"Whatever it is, she is safe now! I'm dying." Hector smiles sadly at me, and my heart falters. "They found cancer a few months ago, and it's spread too far to do anything about it. That's why I went looking for Eric. I couldn't protect you from where I'm headed after everything I've done. I just hope Lucifer will be more merciful than I am to myself."

I just stare at him, his face blurring when tears fill my eyes, but I blink them away, not wanting him to see them. Eric laces his fingers through mine and gives me a reassuring squeeze.

"Michael will stop at nothing to get her, Eric. I don't know the details because they don't trust me anymore. I'm left to die in peace in my own room but stripped from everything I've had." Hector looks from Eric to me. "Even from my daughter as a punishment. Michael wants me to suffer for disobeying him."

"He will not have her," Eric says with so much conviction I honestly believe him.

"Good!" Hector nods, and Eric returns it as if it's some unspoken deal. "George is gathering information for me in the ranks. Come back tomorrow night and he will meet you here. But be careful. I can't know if they'll follow him. Go now!"

I want to stay, to say something meaningful or heartfelt or something, but words escape me. Hector has never been a hugger, but I grab him and squeeze him tight until his arms wrap around me awkwardly, and he pets my head when I release him like I'm some lost puppy. Tears run down my face freely now, but he only nods firmly, first at me, then at Eric, before he disappears through the trees. I let Eric guide me, and I follow him numbly to the SUV, and all the way to his apartment where I curl up, not moving until I fall asleep.

Chapter Twenty-Nine

My body is stiff when I wake up the next morning. I'm still curled up the same way I was when we got to Eric's apartment in the early hours of the dawn. I thought he didn't want to disturb me, so he left me alone, for which I'm grateful, but when I stretch my arms to get rid of the tightness in my muscles, I stop short. I'm curled up on one of the leather couches in his living room. When I uncurl from it, I almost hit his head with my knee, but luckily, I notice him before that happens. He is sitting on the floor, his legs stretched out in front of him with his hands on his stomach, fingers laced together. His head is tilted back on the couch. It looks like

I was curled up around him the whole time I slept. Eric's eyes are closed, and his thick lashes cast shadows on his cheekbones. With his lips slightly parted, he looks so peaceful, all the tension and worry whipped from his face. I sit there and watch him.

"Do I have something on my face?" His voice rumbles, sounding deeper than usual from sleep.

"I was making sure you weren't drooling in your sleep." Snorting ungracefully, I move so he doesn't see my face getting red at being caught staring.

"Are you okay?" Snatching my hand, he doesn't let me get away as he spins me around so we are face to face.

"As good as I can be considering…"

"It'll be okay, I promise. We'll figure it out."

"Don't say that, Eric." Pulling my hand away, I lift myself off the couch. "Michael will never stop coming after me. From what you've told me so far, you have others to worry about and protect. I know you said you'd protect me and reassured me that I'd be okay, but I'm not worth all that trouble, trust me. I'll figure something out. I just need a day or two to do it."

Standing up as well, Eric wraps an arm around my waist and takes a handful of my hair in the other, tilting my head up so I must look at him. "I am the one to decide what is worthwhile to me. And rest assured, you are worth it!" His eyes do that amber flashing thing as he stares intently at me. "He will not have you. I won't allow it!"

"I'm grateful, Eric. Please, don't think I'm not. But he

will kill as many as he needs to until he gets to me. I can't live with that." My eyes soften when I see something like fear before he hides it from me. "It's not that I don't want or need your help. But one life is not worth the cost of many. We both know that."

"Your life is worth all that might get lost in the process to me, Helena. Haven't you figured that out by now?"

"Eric, think about Maddison." I try to reason with him. I'm not even sure why I'm trying to push him to agree to let me go. It's not that I want to be alone. I'm just as afraid that he will get killed while trying to protect me as he is of losing me. "Can you imagine what Michael would do if he gets his hands on her? He will stop at nothing to get me, a half demon. Imagine what he would do to the daughter of Lilith."

"Maddison is a big girl. She can take care of herself." When I take a breath to argue, he kisses me thoroughly, successfully shutting me up and turning my brain to mush.

Picking me up, he starts moving, and I wrap my legs around his waist so he doesn't drop me. I'm not exactly a very skinny girl. My thighs are thick no matter how much training I've done, and my ass is wide enough that he needs more than one hand to get a good grip on it. Yet, he carries me around like I weigh nothing more than a feather, and he's not even breathing heavy. I watch his face while he strides confidently, and although he's not looking at me, his lips twitch, telling me that he is fully aware I'm studying his face. Unable to help myself, I release my grip on his shoulder with one hand and trail my thumb over his full, lower lip. He nips at it, making me jerk it away sharply. He chuckles, causing goosebumps to cover me from head to toe, and I shiver in his arms.

I'm not even jostled as he maneuvers around my ass to open the door to his bedroom and shoulders right in, dumping me on his bed. With a very embarrassing girly squeal, I bounce a couple of times. He laughs, eyes dancing with mirth. When I glower at him, he throws his head back and laughs harder, making me want to do more silly things just to see him like this always. That thought sobers me up.

"I was serious, Eric. Don't try to distract me."

"I was serious too, Helena. You're not going anywhere. We are not helpless little humans who cower before a mighty Archangel. We are demons, and we've been doing this shit with him for a very long time. With, or without you around, nothing will change that." All the laughter is gone from him as he looks down at me.

"He will keep coming, and he will keep attacking. He will never stop fighting to get to me." I point out as a last ditch effort to make him see reason.

"So, we'll fight," he says as nonchalantly as if we are talking about picking apples.

"Eric…" With a tired sigh, I look at him.

"Helena…" he mimics me, and my lips twitch involuntarily.

"Is there anything I can say to make you change your mind about dealing with all the shit that comes with me being around?"

"Yes!" He looks at me with wide eyes. Fear and hope mix together, making me sick to my stomach.

"What is that?" I swallow a couple of times before talking so I can dislodge the lump in my throat.

"Tell me you are a man." At my confused face, he laughs. "I don't bet for the other team, cupcake. So, unless you are a man, you're stuck with me."

Unable to stop myself, I bust out laughing at the stupidity. "You're such an asshole, you know? I actually believed that there really was something." But this isn't a funny situation, so gathering as much courage as I can muster, I look at him. "I thought you might want me to leave. Since I bring so much trouble with me, I wouldn't blame you."

"You might wish I let you go, Hel. But it will never happen. This I can promise you." A shiver runs down my spine from the intensity in his eyes.

"So, what can I do?" At his raised eyebrow, I hurry to explain. "To make this easier for you, I mean."

"Well…" He looks like he is giving it serious thought, so I wait. "To start with, you can take those clothes off so I can see that beautiful body of yours." When my jaw drops at the comment, he chuckles darkly. "I told you, you might wish I let you go. Now take them off before I shred them."

My eyes widen, but he is much faster than me. Before I even blink, he is on me, and the sound of fabric being ripped apart fills my ears.

Chapter Thirty

*P*ressed to the mattress with Eric's weight pinning me down, I claw at his shirt, trying to get rid of it so I can touch his skin. I think he has a lot of patience, but I change my mind when he grabs handfuls of clothing and the sound of tearing fabric mingles with our harsh breathing. Pulling away for a second, he twists around, helping me pull his shirt off before grabbing the sweatpants he let me wear and tearing them at the seams.

I fumble with the belt and buttons on his leather pants when he lifts himself up on his knees to look down at me. I'm now fully naked on his bed, and my legs are spread wide to accommodate his body between them. Getting self-conscious and shy all of a sudden, I release his pants and try to cover myself with my hands, but he grabs my wrists, holding them away from my body. Heat rises up my neck, turning my face red, and I can't even look at him.

"Helena, what are you doing?" Eric's soft voice contrasts with his panting.

"I don't know…" I mumble, staring to the side as if the empty wall is a piece of art. "I feel awkward being naked, and you still half-dressed I guess." My wrists are released, he is off the bed, and what feels like a second later, I hear a thump of metal hitting the floor so my head jerks in that direction.

I forget how to breathe when I see Eric in all his naked glory standing next to the bed, his pants in a heap at his feet. The sound is the buckle hitting the floor. Thickly muscled thighs flex as if he is forcing himself to stand there, and my eyes flick to his. The hunger I see there makes me shiver and my entire body tremble. But he doesn't make a move to come closer, so I shamelessly let my eyes drink him in. His hips are narrow, with a v-line leading to his groin. The very impressive shaft sticking out makes my mouth water as it points up towards the six-pack bunching with his need to both stay still and move. His arms hang at his sides, hands clenched in fists, while his broad shoulders and chest expand with each breath he takes. Finally, I reach his face where his kissable lips are slightly parted, and his nostrils flare while he watches me the same way I'm watching him. Unable to wait any longer, I reach my hand towards him, but he ignores it, pouncing on me instead.

"Thank fuck! I don't think I could've waited longer," he murmurs while frantically kissing my jaw, face, eyelids, and nose. I can't help but laugh. More like giggling, which is stupid really. I don't giggle.

"Okay, okay, I get the idea! You couldn't wait." Pushing on his shoulders, I try to look at his face, but he slides down and latches onto my nipple, making me moan loud and long.

"You were saying?" Eric mumbles, his lips grazing the aching nipple he abandoned so he can speak. Grabbing his hair, I pull him back towards it, making him chuckle darkly before his tongue lashes it. My back bows off the bed.

His hand slides down my side and over my hip before he grabs my thigh, lifting it around his waist. My aching core is pressed to his firm abs, and I grind on him in hopes to quench my need to feel him inside. His cock twitches and bumps my ass cheeks with every movement, reminding me that all I need to do is angle my body right and he will be where I need him most. As if reading my mind, Eric grabs hold of both my hands, lifting them over my head and securing both my wrists in one of his large palms.

"Very impatient!" His eyes look fevered when he gazes down at me.

"Says the guy who just ripped perfectly good sweat

pants and a t-shirt." Panting as much as he is, I manage to speak, but my hips won't stop moving like they have a mind of their own. His cock finally glides between my folds, and he groans deep in his throat, his eyes flashing amber.

"Keep it up and I won't be able to hold myself back. I'm worried I'll rip you apart."

"Have you seen me? I'm not some petite, fragile-looking girl, Eric!" Frowning, I let him see my frustration at not getting what I want. His lips twitch in amusement, the jerk!

"As you wish, Hel." The amusement is gone, replaced with hunger and an intensity that makes me shiver.

Before my brain has time to catch up with the meaning of his words, my wrists are free, and both his hands slide under me, grabbing hold of my ass. Eric's green eyes lock on my wide ones and without any hesitation at all, he pulls back a little, aligning the head of his cock at my entrance before slamming inside me with one jerk of his hips. I am still drenched from just looking at him earlier, so he gets no resistance at all, but he is large enough to give me little pings of pleasure-pain that make my mouth open in a silent scream. My eyes close involuntarily no matter how much I want to keep looking at his face.

Eric snarls and my head snaps up. His face is twisted with a look I've never seen before. His eyebrows are pulled low over his eyes, his upper lip lifts slightly over his clenched teeth, and his eyes are burning fires on his face. His hair looks wild around his head, and his neck has doubled in size with a vein pulsing frantically on one side.

"Hold onto something," he snarls, and I only have time to reach above me and push my fingers under the headboard of the bed.

Eric is a man possessed. Holding my ass in a bruising grip, he sets a frantic tempo, pounding into me so that I can't even keep my thighs around his waist. My legs fall open to the sides, giving him room to do what he wants, and my submission only drives him more insane.

His cock feels like steel wrapped in velvet as he keeps pistoning in and out; I almost forget to breathe at the intensity of it. My breasts bounce wildly from the strength of the pump of his hips, and he buries his face between them, rubbing his stubble like a cat with catnip. The scratchy feeling on my fevered skin adds more power to the rubber band that keeps stretching past its limits inside me. I can't even moan. All I'm capable of doing is holding onto the headboard that will have dents from my fingers and breathe. Eric, on the other hand, keeps grunting, moaning, and snarling, making even me insane wanting to find a way to have him even closer to me where we can become one being.

Without warning, the rubber band snaps and stars burst behind my closed eyelids. It's so much pleasure it borders on pain, but the hold I have on the headboard helps me cling to reality. Eric doesn't stop the punishing tempo, but his snarling and groans get louder. I expect him to join me in the climax of our wild sex, but he doesn't. He keeps pumping his hips without pause, and that rubber band stretches again.

The man is like a machine without a care in the world. I can't even remember how many times I reached my peak and screamed his name from the top of my lungs, making him act even more frantic. I'm barely holding on to reality when the last orgasm hits me full force, and I finally feel him pulsing inside me a split second before a roar that makes my ears ring echoes around the wall. He calls my name. A smile stretches my lips a second before I pass out.

Chapter Thirty - One

Muted voices float through my mushy brain. I'm in that beautiful moment between sleep and being awake, where nothing interferes with the bliss of having your whole body relaxed and your mind silent. It doesn't last long, but I enjoy it while I can. Then the severity of real life and all the problems that come with it slowly sucks the joy out of me slowly. My body is deliciously sore, and I know I have bruises all over, so nothing stops the satisfied smile that stretches my lips while my eyes are still closed. Footsteps sound outside the door a moment before it opens, but I keep my eyes closed, not willing to face reality just yet.

"Morning, cupcake!" Eric sounds too chirpy and so

unlike himself that I open one eye to wishing I can stab him with a look, and to make sure it really is him.

"If you call me a cupcake one more time, I'm going to shove my gun up your ass and pull the trigger," I mumble with only one eye open. He throws his head back and laughs. Even after last night, my channel clenches at the sight of him.

"Fair enough." He smiles and sits on the side of the bed, pushing my hair out of my face. "But it got you awake and talking. It's a good tactic." He winks at me.

"Who are you and what did you do to Eric?" Opening my other eye, I look at him with a serious expression.

"Can't a man be in a good mood without being questioned?" Raising one eyebrow, he acts hurt, and I can't fight the smile that's trying to lift my lips.

"A man can. A demon, on the other hand, makes you wonder." Sticking out my tongue at him, I squeal when he lunges forward and tickles me. "Okay, okay, stop!"

"Come on, Maddison is here." After kissing me softly on the lips, he helps me untangle myself from the covers.

His hands freeze, and he stiffens when I stand in front of him. Looking at the horror on his face, I follow his eyes to see what's got him so freaked out. My hips have purplish, green handprints on them and a burst of laughter bubbles out. Eric looks at me like I've finally lost my mind.

"My skin bruises easily, Eric. I promise I'm fine." Smiling, I cup his face while he searches my eyes to see if

I'm telling him the truth, nostrils flaring and all. "It was worth it, and I'll do it again." His eyes turn hungry at that comment, but I push him towards the door. "I'll be out in a minute, go!"

He grumbles something under his breath that I don't catch but leaves me to freshen up and get ready for whatever kind of day this turns out to be. The shower feels heavenly, and with a sigh, I eye the small pool that acts like a bathtub in longing. Twisting my wet hair in a bun, I rummage through the duffle bag Hector gave me last night and pull out clothing. I'm grateful I can wear my own clothes instead of Eric's. Not that I mind being engulfed in his scent all day, but I feel more like myself this way. When I find my travel bag with my makeup inside, my heart clenches. I push it away and hurry to get ready before the emotion makes me curl up and cry for as long as I have tears in me. I can't afford that time right now.

"Good morning," I announce my presence as soon as I step into the living room. Maddison looks at me over her shoulder with a smile.

"Helena! Good morning." My feet slow down at her too enthusiastic greeting, and I look at Eric for help, but the jerk is avoiding my eyes.

"Okay…" Dragging out the word, I walk up to one of the couches across from Eric and plop down. "Do we have any good news?"

"What do you mean?" Maddison is practically

bouncing in her seat, and Eric groans, which tells me whatever it is I'm not going to like it. "It's the best news I've had in centuries! Who would've thought—"

"Maddison, stop!" Eric snaps, and my eyes narrow at him while Madison trails off, looking at both of us in turn with wide, blue eyes. Her mouth forms a pretty little circle, and her eyebrows go up to her hairline.

"What is going on, Eric?"

Someone knocks on the front door, and it opens, but none of us look away from each other to see who it is.

"You didn't tell her that she's your mate?" Maddison's eyes narrow, but Eric is staring straight at me and doesn't miss when the blood drains from my face.

"I'm your what now?"

"She's your what now?" Whoever joined us speaks at the same time as me, and we all turn to see Loren staring at Eric with wide eyes while all the color drains from her face as if it's her ass being claimed as property.

"I can't deal with this right now," I tell the room in general, and with a groan, I sink into the soft couch, covering my face with my hands.

The room is silent for few moments before the click-click of high heels on the floor makes me move my hands to see Loren come up to Maddison and hands her a black folder a couple of inches thick. After glaring at me, she turns and practically glides out of the apartment. After she closes the front door with a loud bang, I look at Eric. He hasn't taken his eyes off me and sits as still as a statue.

"I guess you two need to talk about this." Maddison starts moving as if she's planning to leave and I panic.

"No!" At my outburst, Eric growls, but I hurry to explain before this turns into an argument. "We can talk about it later. Please, is there anything you've found out? I think getting Michael and the Order off our back first is more important."

Maddison, to my surprise, doesn't look like she agrees with me. Uneasiness tries to gnaw a hole in my stomach, but I push it away. It seems like it's going to be one of those days, so I'll just go with the flow and suppress as many emotions as I can. Reluctantly, Maddison opens the folder and starts pulling out photos of some sort of a farm.

"What's this?" Scooting closer to the edge of the couch, I try to get a better look at the photos.

"It's how our hideout used to look." At my confused face, she tries to explain. "Decades ago, we bought this land and rebuilt it, turning it into a sanctuary. We have some of our kind living there behind wards where the hunters or angels can't bother them. They are free to leave, but most of them stay and help us to keep things under the human's radar."

"So, why are you showing me this?" Confused, I look from her to Eric. My heart skips a beat when I realize he hasn't moved a muscle and is still staring at me.

"I'm not showing you. I brought these to show Eric. The wards are strong, but if we are to have you behind them, I thought strengthening them might be a good idea. That's why I needed the original plans of the place."

"We will go there now and figure things out on the spot," Eric tells Maddison without looking away from me. It's unnerving.

"Okay, perfect!" She practically jumps off the couch after shoving the photos in the folder without caring if they get crumpled or not and runs out the door. I don't miss the look she gives Eric, mouthing sorry before the front door closes behind her.

"Eric…"

Ignoring me, he stands up and starts walking out of the apartment. I don't know what to do, so I just watch him until he is halfway out the door.

"Let's go!" he says without turning, and I follow behind him with a ton of bricks sitting in my stomach.

Chapter Thirty-Two

We take the drive in a tense silence with me not knowing what to say and Eric clutching the steering wheel like he wants to take all his anger out on it. Now that I've had time to think about it and since the shock has worn off, the fact that he thinks I'm his mate warms me inside. I'm also aware my reaction hurt him, so here I am having full conversations in my head looking at something that sounds close to a sincere apology. If our roles were reversed, I would've been mortified seeing him react the way I did and I'm not totally sure I would've been willing to hear his apology.

I still haven't come up with the right words when we near what looks like a closed off junkyard. The metal fence around it looks rusted, and I rub my hands over my arms at the thought of being around the nastiness I can see in piles all over the place. Eric drives straight at the double doors of the gate, and pulling a remote out of the glovebox, presses a button, opening it. He makes sure he doesn't touch me while he does it, and I feel like crying or screaming at him that I'm sorry. Swallowing the lump, I say nothing.

After the gate opens just enough for us to drive through it, Eric hits the gas and drives in. As soon as we are past the gates, my view changes and I'm staring at a building almost as large as the sanctuary, only this one looks more like a hunting lodge. Built from thick pieces of wood, it looks inviting and makes me feel at ease straight away. The dark green roof compliments the bright red front door, making it look beautiful. It's an understatement to say that I'm impressed.

People—well demons, in this case—walk around, some clustered in groups chatting. It almost looks surreal, like a scene from a movie showing life in a secluded community—which I suppose this really is when you look at it that way. As we near the clusters of people, they turn to look. Some smile, while others raise a hand in greeting. Eric drives up to another parked SUV, taking the spot next to it, and without waiting on me, he jumps out of the car as soon as the engine cuts off.

With a sigh, I turn to open the door while pulling my seatbelt off. I'm surprised when my door opens and Eric takes hold of my arm, helping me jump down from the high vehicle. What's more surprising is that he doesn't let go when my feet touch the ground. His hand glides down my arm and interlaces our fingers. I look at his face and hope blooms that maybe I didn't screw this up as bad as I thought I did.

"Oh, you did, but I'll make you pay for it in other ways," Eric murmurs and I realize I must've spoken out loud.

"I really am sorry for the way I reacted," I tell him honestly. "I was shocked more than upset I guess."

"Shocked at what? Being my mate?" One eyebrow lifts up, and his intense scrutiny makes me squirm.

"At being trapped?" Huffing, I look away from his penetrating gaze "At not having the option to choose things of my own free will?"

"You sound like my father." At his words, I look sharply at him, making him chuckle. "He goes on and on about free will and such."

"Not funny!" Hitting him in the stomach with the back of my hand, I make him laugh again.

"It was funny to see the look on your face. Come on." Grabbing my hand again, he pulls me towards the large home. "Let's see what we can do here before we have to leave to meet with your friend George."

My gut clenches at the mention of George and the Order, but I say nothing as he leads me around the place. The inside is as beautiful as the outside, and Eric tells me

Maddison is the one who decorates and purchases things for the home. I would've guessed it without him pointing it out. Everything looks measured and elegant, just like her. Eric talks to people, answers questions thrown his way, and keeps gliding like he owns the place. I stay quiet, lost in my head, and follow behind him like a shadow. Some of the demons nod at me, others look at me suspiciously, but no one asks who I am or what I'm doing here. The enigma of that is solved when Maddison pops out of nowhere.

"Ah! You're finally here!" She walks up to us and snatches my hand from Eric's. He growls low in his chest, but she returns it with a bright smile. "Go fix the wards, cousin. I'll keep your girl occupied until you're done." It seems like she yells the words because silence follows them, and everyone's eyes turn to me, making my face turn all shades of red.

"I won't be long." Eric tugs me to his chest and kisses me softly on the lips. "Stay with Maddison."

Maddison sighs dreamily, and my face goes from warm to burning.

I watch Eric's back as he walks away with two men as tall as him. "You're not helping, Maddison," I mumble as I press the backs of my hands to my cheeks.

"I can't help it!" She takes my hand, dragging me further into the home. "I'm a romantic at heart. And seeing Eric, the king of no commitment, with a mate makes me want to go on the roof and scream it to the world." She stops her rapid fire of words and turns to look at me with a serious face. "I'll scream 'suck on this, assholes! Love always wins!'"

I burst out laughing at the excited look on her face. It's even funnier coming from her since she always acts all prim and proper. You'd think she was the one raised in the Order, not me.

We spend our time talking about random things, and Maddison tells me little stories about Eric and their antics through the centuries. It's so easy to forget how old they are when they look my age, or maybe a couple of years older. At twenty-one, I'm not even at toddler status when it comes to these guys. There is a moment when it feels like ants are crawling all over my skin, but she assures me it's because Eric is checking the wards before he places stronger ones over them. I have no reason to worry looking at the smiling faces outside the window of the cozy little room where we are sitting. Maddison visibly stiffens a moment before the ground shakes with such force I think it must be an earthquake. When I look at her face, I realize we must be screwed. Before I have a chance to ask what's going on, another rumble almost makes me fall off the sofa. When it stops, something crashes somewhere inside the home before I hear Eric's roar.

"Helena!"

Chapter Thirty-Three

"Helena!" The second time Eric bellows my name, my blood turns to ice. Something is terribly wrong.

Maddison jumps to her feet just as the door bangs open. It bounces off the opposite wall and tilts to the side when the top hinge doesn't manage to hold its weight. Eric storms in, looking like a crazy man with wild eyes that zero in on me. His chest is heaving like he's been running, but I know he doesn't get winded like that. In two strides he is in front of me, snatching me around the waist and turning to sprint out.

"What's going on?" Maddison and I speak at the same time.

"The wards are down." Eric turns his head to look at Maddison, stopping for a moment. "The entire Order is at our gates."

"Go!" Maddison pushes Eric to move and she bolts out of the room so fast I didn't see her cross the space to the door before her red hair disappears through it.

"Out of all the days, I don't have my guns today." My words pass my numb lips as my mind screams that this is all my fault.

"You don't need them because you're not fighting." Snarling the words, he lifts me off the ground, and, holding me to his chest, starts running towards the front door.

I cling to him like a spider monkey, unable to stop him if I try while he barrels through the panicked people in the hallways. There is screaming and cussing, people yelling words I can't hear from the buzzing in my ears and the strange numbness that overtakes my entire being. Eric doesn't stop for anything. He doesn't even seem to care about anyone else but me and my guilt skyrockets. All this is my fault, and instead of helping his kind survive, he's trying to get my shocked ass out of here. That thought gets my blood pumping, and anger stews in my chest.

"Put me down!" I have to yell to be heard even when my head is close to his. Eric ignores me, so I punch his shoulder to get his attention. "Put me down! I can fight!"

"No!" Snarling, he keeps running until we exit the front doors to a scene out of a movie.

There is a wall of hunters around the entire place just standing there, unmoving, their weapons ready in their hands. Three rows of hunters, one behind the other, stand unnaturally still as if in some sort of trance, while all around me chaos makes faces blur as they run in panic. Eric stops dead in his tracks, drops my feet on the ground, and pushes me behind his back. In my anger, I thump my fist on his back for being so stubborn, but there is nothing much I can do when he stands as an unmovable rock in front of me.

Just when I think we are doomed, Maddison strides from the side of the large home with a horde of demons the size of Abaddon following at her heels. She doesn't look one bit fazed by the Order's display, and she even has a smile on her face. I think the beautiful woman that I've started to admire has finally lost her mind. Swaying her hips, she glides towards us and stops next to Eric. Her entourage positions themselves like a living fence in front of us and faces the hunters. The crazy screaming and running around stops and I watch stupefied when the panicked demons, one by one, start joining the horned ones and grab whatever they can find to use as a weapon.

"You can at least show yourself, Michael." Maddison calls out, making me wince. "I promise I won't bite… much!" While she talks, I manage to slide from behind Eric and stand at his side. He doesn't look happy, but tough luck for him.

"Maddison," Michael's smooth voice rings out before

I even see him in the distance, the hunters parting for him like some creepy choreographed display. "This has nothing to do with you. I just want the girl."

"Aww, that's where we have a problem, handsome." She pouts prettily at him, almost making me smile. "So does my cousin."

"What?" Michael sounds confused, and so am I.

"Eric." Maddison flicks her thumb in Eric's direction. "He wants the girl, too." Her smile brightens up her whole face. The woman is definitely crazy.

"Helena, when the fight starts, I need you to run to the car," Eric murmurs under his breath, and I gape at him. He wants me to run and leave them to die for me?

"I'm not playing games, Maddison." Michael bellows, his face reddening in anger. "I will take the girl. If the rest of you live or die in the process, it's totally up to you."

Ignoring everyone, including Eric who is glaring daggers at me, I start looking around to see if there is anything I can use as a weapon. I mean how hard can it be? These are not demons I need to fight. They are hunters, like me. That makes them human and easy to hurt. I was best in all my training for a reason. None of them could beat my scores, and it's time to remind them why. Seeing what looks like a shovel leaning on the side of the house, I slink up to it, and stepping on the metal part, I pull as hard as I can, breaking off the handle. Twirling it in my hands, I glance up to see Eric looking at me with raised eyebrows.

"Playtime." I twirl it again. Maddison's laughter makes my smile grow bigger, and finally, Eric's lips twitch.

"Kill them all and get the girl alive." Michael's angry bellow makes everyone move at once.

Hunters swarm us from all sides. Sounds of fists hitting flesh and metal and wood bouncing off each other echoes, followed by yells and screams of anger and pain. I don't leave Eric's side, and neither does Maddison. The two of us guard his back as he sends one hunter after another to the ground, and they don't stand up again. I'm hoping they are unconscious and not dead, but since our lives are in danger, I don't have it in me to care too much.

I have no idea where she found it, but Maddison is wielding a beautifully carved short sword with a jeweled handle that twinkles in the daylight. There is no blood on it, yet, so I'm guessing she uses it more to hit them than stab them.

"I wonder how they found us here." Eric grunts angrily as he punches yet another poor soul in the face, knocking him down. "I know we were not followed."

"Does it matter?" I ask as I whack one on the head who tries to grab at me. He totters for a moment before dropping on the ground like a rock. He will have a horrible headache when he wakes up.

"Yes." Eric and Maddison answer at the same time.

We continue fighting, but after a while, they manage to pull us away from each other. There are just so many hunters, and there is not a moment to stop and take a breath. They just keep coming. I lose sight of both Eric and Maddison, so I concentrate on keeping the hunters away from me. Twist, turn, smack across any part of the body, stop. And repeat. It's almost calming when it's a constant repetition of the same. That is my downfall this day.

I am so concentrated on repeating my movements that it takes me longer to realize that they stop coming. A second too late, I hear the whoosh of air above me before two arms grab me around my waist and my feet leave the ground.

I feel dazed at being airborne and can't do anything but hang like a deadweight. Eric's roar snaps me out of it, and swinging my handle, I hit whoever it is as hard as I can, breaking the wood in half. The arms holding me release, and I have a second for my mind to scream *Oh, shit!* before I plummet to the ground.

My life flashes before me as I brace myself for the impact with the ground, but it doesn't happen. My flailing body is snatched in the air like some weird game a bird would play with a worm. After a second, I'm unceremoniously dropped on the ground. My stomach rebels with all the flying and dropping, so I bend over with my hands on my knees and empty it all over a pair of shiny black shoes.

"Oh, for goodness sake." Michael's voice sounds

disgusted, and I can't say I blame him. Regardless of that, I smile because I'm so proud of myself for messing up his perfect appearance.

"Oops…" Wiping my mouth with the back of my hand, I give him the biggest smile ever. He backhands me, making my head fly to the side, and I taste blood when my lip splits.

"Helena!" Eric's scream rips my heart apart, but I can't look his way. It'll kill me if I do. Michael is here for me, and if he has me, he will leave them alone so I won't fight him. "Michael, I would give her back if I were you."

"She doesn't look like she wants to go back." Michael gloats when he sees that I'm not fighting him.

"I don't give a fuck what she seems like, you piece of shit! Give her back now." Eric is still fighting hordes of hunters, but his eyes are glued on me.

I forget all about Michael and Eric when another man pops out of nowhere behind Michael. His hair is brown, cut similarly as Michael's, and he shares the same porcelain skin and perfect angelic face. But his eyes are different. His yellow, cat-like eyes watch me curiously, and there is kindness in them that almost makes me weep. He nods once at me, placing a finger over his lips as if telling me not to oust him, and then puts a fist over his heart.

"Raphael, it took you long enough," Michael snaps, not even looking behind him.

"You are making a mistake, brother." Raphael's voice is soft, but deep, putting me at ease.

"I didn't ask you for advice. Just keep them busy until I take her away." A snarling Michael grabs my arm, pulling me towards him, and as if hypnotized, I don't fight him. I can't take my eyes off Raphael.

"If you take her, I promise you that you will die." Eric's voice has so much power packed in it that I feel it burning my skin.

"Yeah, yeah," Michael mutters. "Nothing I haven't heard before."

"It's not smart to piss off the Prince of Hell before you take his mate," Raphael says as if he is talking about a cookie recipe.

"Wha…" My question is cut off when Michael presses a spot on my neck and my eyes roll to the back of my head. The last thought I have is, *Oh my God, Eric is the Prince of Hell.* I never made the connection, and hearing his terrifying roar, I feel sorry for whoever will be the recipient of his anger.

To be continued

C ontinue the story in Book 2, click the link.
Speak of the Devil Book 2

ABOUT THE AUTHOR

Rebel,

You survived being inside my head, and I salute you for the bravery! I'm grateful for you, and I hope you enjoyed the start of the journey Helena and Eric are taking, as much as I enjoyed writing it. The story will go up and down, and when you think you finally get it, it'll flip on you at the last moment. Even when it seems they are taking a step back, there is a good reason for it, and I hope you'll keep up with their adventures until the very end. The fight against Michael continues in "Speak of the Devil". The link is on the next page.

If you loved reading the story, please take a moment to leave a review. If you like to stay updated on my new releases or giveaways, sign up for the newsletter. I reply to every single one of you, so don't be afraid to drop me a line...or two.

Sign up here

Come stalk me on FB, I love talking to you guys.

Happy reading!

Maya xxx

Printed in Great Britain
by Amazon

58707781R00139